HERO 1: RISE OF THE HEROES

ANDY BRIGGS

TANGLEBOX

BOOKS

BOOK 1

RISE OF THE HEROES

HERO 1: RISE OF THE HEROES

Copyright © 2020 by Andy Briggs

www.andybriggsbooks.com
Twitter: @abriggswriter
Instagram: @itsandybriggs

For Dad
An inspiration forever

FROZEN_

THE C-3 TRANSPORT plane bucked against the invisible eddies that swirled around the aircraft, metres above the earth. The Hercules was the workhorse of the air force, but it had not been designed to take the kind of punishment that was hammering it now.

The malevolent storm had appeared from blue skies. Snow pelted the craft and choked the four powerful engines - one of which was still aflame from the missile impact - forcing it rapidly to lose airspeed and precious altitude. Below, the bleak continent of Antarctica beckoned to the Hercules's passengers with a sub-zero embrace.

Inside, two twelve-year-old boys, Toby and Pete, gripped the safety harnesses bolted to their jump-seats, their knuckles white as the plane belly-flopped. Any items not secured jumped into the air and remained there, held in a curious state of zero gravity as they nosedived towards the earth. Toby thought he was going to be sick for sure.

Having watched countless documentaries on the television he remembered the term 'parabola': NASA flew planes towards the earth to simulate zero-G. They were affectionately known as 'Vomit Comets'. And that's exactly how he felt now, feeling the bile rise in his throat. They would have about forty seconds of this nauseating feeling before the plane crashed into the ground. And after everything that had happened this week, he was pretty sure they wouldn't survive that.

All these thoughts flitted through Toby's mind in a second. He smashed open the restraining clip on his safety harness and floated out into the cargo area of the aircraft just like he'd seen astronauts do on television. Pete watched Toby free-float out and unbuckled his own belt to join him. Unable to precisely control his movements, Toby rotated upside-down, his inverted perspective disorienting him further.

Thirty seconds to impact . . .

'We have to open the rear doors!' yelled Toby over the monstrous droning of the Allison Turboprop engines.

Pete looked around frantically. 'The release switch is automated. It's in the cockpit!'

'Dammit!' cried Toby. They both knew there was no time to break through into the fortified cockpit and override the drone pilot controls.

Twenty-five seconds.

Toby kicked himself away from the bulkhead, and soared towards the rear of the aircraft, steadying himself as he flew over pallets held in place with canvas webbing. He knew once they opened the door the supply pallets would create an additional problem.

Pete tried to use his arms to swim through the air; instead he revolved uselessly on the spot.

Toby cried over to him. 'I can't do this! This is your area of expertise!'

Pete threw out a hand and steadied himself by catching the pallet webbing.

'Blast the doors and use the pallets to spring out!' cried Toby.

That was the problem with flying; it was difficult to do if you were plummeting. You needed a springboard to push yourself upwards. Even with superpowers, physics always butted its unwelcome nose in.

Twenty . . .

Pete laboriously heaved himself over to Toby. Both boys planted their feet against the pallets; coiled for action. Pete removed his glasses - he had long learnt his lesson - and focused on the rear cargo door that opened like a jaw under the Hercules's tail section.

BAM! A concentrated beam of blue energy leapt from his eyes and blew the cargo door into twisted metal fragments. Frigid winds sucked at the aircraft's contents.

The sudden loss of pressure pulled the contents of the craft out with teeth-jarring speed. The pallets vaulted under their feet, rocketing the teenagers out into the blizzard. Inertia pushed them flat against the boxes underfoot but both boys knew they had to push upwards; otherwise they would simply crash into the ground with the rest of the aircraft.

Using every part of their remaining strength, they pushed - and suddenly they found themselves flying up, away from the aircraft and its cargo of supply pallets–

And towards the jagged mountains!

No sooner had they taken flight, than the Hercules smashed forcibly into the side of the mountain. Pete's mental countdown had not taken account of the fact that the ground had swept up in the form of the Neptune Mountain Range to meet them.

The Hercules transport erupted into a vivid orange fireball. Twenty freefalling pallets impacted into the inferno seconds later. Toby could feel the flames licking his heels, but he urged himself to fly faster, throwing out both arms before him, just in case that assisted.

Out of the corner of his eye, he saw Pete banking downwards, away from the fireball's path. Toby lost no time in joining him.

They arced around and down in a flight path that a military jock would term a 'yo-yo manoeuvre'. Within seconds the steeply sloping, icy flanks of the mountain were underneath them and the Hercules was lost from visibility in the storm.

The cold bit hard, zapping Toby's energy even through the multilayered thermal gear that covered almost every centimetre of him. He knew he had no choice but to land firmly on the mountain slope, or risk dropping from the sky and rolling the rest of the way downhill. A quick glance confirmed Pete was thinking the same.

Toby pivoted so he was no longer aiming headfirst down the mountain. He slowed, dropping the last metre to the ground. He fell on all fours to keep his balance, and sank to his knees and elbows. Pete landed next to him. Already the driving blizzard had coated them with a layer of frost.

Pete's teeth chattered. 'That . . . was a new experience, huh?'

Before Toby could reply a noise got his attention. It was bass-heavy, countering the wind's tremolo. The ground beneath them shook; with a feeling of dreadful realization, Toby turned his gaze uphill.

The flaming carcass of the aircraft was sledging down the hill, and gaining momentum with every second.

'Watch out!' screamed Toby.

He had no time to push his friend aside, and no strength to take flight again. Instead he could only leap sideways with the very last of his ebbing strength.

His face was buried in the snow as he landed, and the world shook around him as the burning twisted debris thundered past like a runaway locomotive. He remained motionless as, seconds later, he was pelted with smaller detritus that bounced off his protective gear. Toby was certain that, had he not been wearing the multiple layers, a jagged piece of shrapnel would have cut him open.

The ground stopped trembling and the driving wind howled some more. Toby picked himself up and looked wildly around.

Pete had gone.

'Pete! Where are you?'

Panic seized him, overriding the permeating chill. He staggered forward.

'Pete! Please?'

He looked hopelessly around, and then dropped to his knees. With every ounce of self-control, he stopped himself from crying; tears would freeze over his eyeballs in the -50 Celsius atmosphere and no doubt blind him.

If the aircraft had struck Pete then he would surely be dead. Pete's current range of superpowers would do nothing to save him from being crushed by a flaming aircraft.

Dead. Maybe like Lorna, Emily . . . and his mother.

Toby shook the dark thoughts from his mind and assessed his situation. It was almost as stark. He was two thousand miles away from the nearest civilization, which was located on the tip of Argentina, trapped at over a thousand feet on the snow-covered peak.

Storm force winds promised to spirit him away if he dared fly again - not that he had the strength.

His best friend was probably dead. His sister and her friend had been caught, and a madman held his mother captive: an unspeakably evil villain who had demolished Fort Knox in the United States.

And it seemed Toby was the only person who could now save the world from disaster.

Talk about a bad week.

Toby reflected on how the last seven days had transformed their lives beyond imagination. In one moment he and his friends had turned from teenagers into superheroes. The innocence of their youth had been stripped raw.

Everything had changed the day they chanced on the source of their extraordinary powers . . .

THE STORM_

It was cold, but crystal blue skies offered a perfect day for shoot 'em tag in the forest that stood at the end of the road. Brown fronds crunched noisily underfoot, but the flaxen leaves that still clung to the trees offered just enough cover to hide. As usual the game between Toby and Pete was fast and furious. Toby was the more athletic of the two, and pressed his advantage by sprinting through the trees, leaving Pete exhausted by the time he caught up. Plus, Pete was never a good shot. In fact, had the gun been a high energy laser, rather than a toy, half the trees in the forest would have been on fire. Now *that* would be fun.

But after almost an hour of punishing combat, the sky had glowered. Bloated clouds rolled across the sun and brought a heavy shower that forced the boys to retreat from the forest. The autumns had become increasingly erratic thanks to their parents' legacy of global warming. By the time they reached the garden gate the shower had bloomed into a torrential downpour that hammered a rhythmic tattoo against the garden furniture.

And the back door was locked from the inside.

'Lorna!' yelled Toby as he rattled the handle and thumped on the wooden frame, flakes of old paint floating to the ground. 'It's raining! Open up!'

Pete had caught him up and joined Toby in beating the door. 'Why's it locked?' he asked, cold raindrops dripping across his glasses and blurring his vision.

'My sister, that's why.'

On cue, shrill laughter from the window above got their attention. Lorna brushed her long dark hair from across her face as she watched her brother's predicament. A flash of blonde hair appeared alongside to watch with equally wicked amusement: Emily.

'Getting wet?' taunted Lorna. 'Not a good day to be stuck outside.'

Toby stood back, waving his plastic rifle in frustration. 'Oh, very witty. Very clever. You'll pass your exams in a flash with comments like that!'

Pete was not as adept in sarcasm as his friend and shouted, 'Can't you see we're soaked?'

Lorna was unmoved. 'Serves you both right!'

Pete scowled. 'What've I done?'

'Not letting us join in your stupid game,' chided Lorna.

The rain was coming down harder; fat drops slapped their faces. And each strike infuriated Toby. 'If it's so stupid, then why are you upset?'

'Upset? Do I sound upset? I'm having a great time! I'm in here, nice and warm. And dry.'

Toby held back his angry reply; he didn't want to risk aggravating his sister. He swapped a glance with Pete who knew what was coming next. The ultimate weapon.

'If you don't let us in right now . . . then I'll tell Mum when she gets back.'

'A bit old for that, aren't we?'

So maybe the 'ultimate weapon' didn't apply as much when you're twelve, or in Lorna's case, an unscrupulous thirteen and a bit.

'Looks like you're stuck!' said Emily with delight.

Lorna nodded. 'And after all the stupid jokes you two have played on us, nothing's going to change our minds.'

No sooner had the words slipped from her mouth than a jagged lightning bolt stabbed the ground with multiple forks, blasting a pair of heavy branches off a solid oak tree that had dominated the garden for over a hundred years. With a terrifying crack of electricity, fragments of wood shot across the grass.

Lorna blanched, looking up in shock. Toby and Pete spun round; the smell of charred wood invaded their nostrils as several scarred branches crashed to the floor in a shower of embers just a few metres away.

Toby's scalp was red by the time Lorna had finished vigorously towelling it dry. Now his hair pointed in every direction, as if he'd been electrocuted.

'Stop it! It hurts,' complained Toby as he pushed Lorna back.

'I said I'm sorry!' sighed Lorna. And to her surprise she actually was. Like most siblings, she and Toby fought occasionally (or constantly if you listened to their parents), but it was never too serious.

The four of them sat around the large, solid-timber kitchen table, with a bottle of cola standing open. Pete refilled his glass for the fourth time, pausing only to belch loudly.

'You almost killed us out there!' accused Toby.

Lightning licked across the heavens as if to emphasize his point. It was now a tempest outside, the sky as dark as charcoal.

'Which means we're stuck with each other in here,' warned Lorna.

Pete and Emily exchanged a surreptitious glance.

They had long watched their friends bicker - and while they openly supported them, inside they wished they'd both just get it over with. Some disagreements had been known to continue for days. And this was just the kind of thing Pete would rather avoid.

'Well, just keep out of my way and we'll be fine,' said Toby.

'No more arguments.'

'Fine. We'll do our own thing.'

'Good,' said Toby sullenly .

'There are lots of things we can still do inside.'

There was a pregnant pause.

Lorna's and Toby's eyes locked as though reading one another's thoughts. Toby's leg muscles tensed, and by the time he was on his feet Lorna had already bolted ahead of him through the kitchen door.

Like her brother, Lorna enjoyed sports, in particular cross-country running. But Toby had the advantage in short-distance sprints and he shoved her against the wall as they passed in the hallway, leaving her shouting after him as he entered their father's study.

'Toby! Stop! That's so not fair!'

Emily and Pete followed in their wake, eager to join the chase but unaware of their destination.

The study was lined with reference books, framed maps, and photographs of exotic destinations, souvenirs from their father's constant travelling. A heavy desk, the size of a wardrobe, sat in front of massive bay windows offering an impressive view of the garden and the angry storm.

Toby vaulted the side of the desk and slipped straight into the comfortable leather reclining chair, situated directly in front of a large monitor. He stabbed the desktop computer's power button as Lorna sprinted into the study and sat heavily on his lap, knocking the breath from him.

'Get off it!' Lorna shouted, and punched his arm for emphasis.

'Why should I?' said Toby, trying to push her off with little success. He swallowed the comment he was about to make about Lorna feeling heavier. He knew mentioning her weight would turn the situation nuclear.

Pete and Emily had now entered the room as the elderly computer booted up, its cooling fan noisily whirling away inside.

Lorna pressed her weight harder on Toby's stomach before she climbed off him. 'Emily and I were going to use that!' she protested.

Toby grinned as the loading tune played from the computer's speakers. 'Tough. I was here first. You could've used it while we were outside.'

This was a battle as old as time. They'd pleaded for their own computers, then begged for their own phones, but their parents had refused. At first complaining about cost of something that would be out of date a year later, then pointing out they'd break them. Their mother was a nut when it came to how much screen-time they had. At least Emily and Pete both had their own machines at home. Life wasn't fair.

Toby's hand had already manoeuvred the mouse so he could select the browser icon. Two clicks and the broadband connection took him online as thunder boomed outside.

'We have homework to do!' protested Emily.

'Well go do it then,' said Pete smugly as he dragged a high-backed wooden chair across to sit by Toby.

Emily glared at him. 'I meant on the computer.' But Toby and Pete already had their noses in the browser, scrutinizing the numerous links on the colourful homepage that had loaded.

'Check out the movie trailers,' said Pete, placing a greasy fingerprint on the screen as he pointed to the link. He glanced up at Emily. 'If you've homework to do, don't you have a tablet at home?'

Emily shrugged her head. She also had an older brother at home who preferred using it, and she was used to having to fight to get her own way. Pete's attitude annoyed her. It always seemed to change around Toby. When he was alone with her they had fun and he was always looking out for her. But as soon as Toby entered the equation Pete would side with him no matter what. She wasn't going to allow him to get his own way this time.

She opened her mouth to respond - as lightning lit up the room like a flashbulb. A second later thunder clapped the air with astonishing fury, making them all jump.

'Storm's getting worse,' warned Emily.

Lorna followed her gaze outside as she had a troubling thought.

'Toby, I don't think you should be on the phone during a thunderstorm.'

Toby didn't look up, as a series of the latest Hollywood movie trailers appeared on-screen. 'We're not on the phone. We're online.'

'Yeah, but it still uses the phone line, stupid.' She didn't want to add they'd also lost the plea for cable and a faster connection/

Pete looked up at her, his mouth forming the words to agree. But whatever sound came out was masked by a blinding flash of lightning and a simultaneous sonorous roll of thunder that made the pictures on the wall rattle as if a bomb had exploded outside.

Which was close to what had actually happened.

Lorna saw the jagged fork of lightning lick the top of the telegraph pole at the end of the garden, and when she closed her eyes she still had the ghostly after-image imprinted on her eyeball. None of them saw the electric bolt crackle along the phone cable towards the house.

The computer made a high-pitched death rattle before the screen went blank.

Pete's heart was hammering from the momentary excitement. 'Wow! That was close!'

Lorna shook her head. 'It struck the telephone pole. Look, it killed the computer.'

Toby stared at the blank screen in horror. 'Oh, God, no. Not now.'

A vengeful smile tugged Lorna's lips. 'Dad is going to kill you for breaking his computer! All his work is on it!'

Toby blanched and felt a sudden sickness in the pit of his stomach. Lorna was right. Their father was an archaeologist and, as far as Toby knew, all his research was stored on the hard drive, he never backed anything up.

'Dad's not even in the country!' He wondered where exactly he was; somewhere in Mexico, Mum had said.

His work meant that it was usual for him to disappear for weeks on end with only a satellite phone for communication, and that was usually temperamental at best.

'Lightning could have blown a fuse, or maybe the power pack!' said Emily.

Pete looked at her sceptically. 'Oh, you're a tech expert all of a sudden?'

Emily rolled her eyes and tried to hide her smile.

Pete examined the casing. 'Listen. The fan's still on. Maybe it's just the screen that's bust?'

Toby thumbed the monitor's power button with a faint trace of hope. His spirits lifted as an image slowly returned to the screen.

'Thank God!' he said, breathing out a huge sigh of relief. He flicked a victorious look at his sister. 'It's not dead.'

Lorna pulled a face. 'Well, you should get off it before you do break it.'

Not willing to chance his luck any further, Toby reluctantly agreed. 'Point taken.'

His hand found the mouse, guiding it across the desktop to shut the system down. Pete suddenly grabbed his wrist to stop him.

'Wait! That's not the website we were on before.'

The movie trailers had been replaced by a completely different set of icons and text, all of it unfamiliar.

'So? You'd still better turn it off,' warned Lorna.

Toby waved his hand to silence her. 'Hold on, Lorn. Take a look. This is weird.'

Lorna and Emily crowded next to the boys. A bold banner filled the top of the screen: "HERO".

'This another of your stupid comic book sites?' Emily asked.

Pete pointed to the screen, leaving a new greasy splodge where his finger had been. 'Look at the URL.'

'WWW.Geekybrother, by any chance?' said Lorna smugly.

'No .com or anything. Weird, it's not like a proper address." The address bar on the screen was filled with a series of strange characters that constantly shifted and changed. 'What kind of site is Hero?' asked Lorna.

'One that's not on the Internet,' said Toby ominously as another flash of lightning and a thunder roll indicated the storm was retreating. But the rain outside drummed more heavily.

Underneath the banner, a series of four icons stood out. Toby passed the pointer over each, but other than the enigmatic title, there was not another word in English . . . or any other language for that matter.

'Click on something,' urged Pete.

'OK. The first icon, I suppose,' said Toby, motioning towards a swirling whirlpool. He clicked and moments later the webpage changed to another series of icons. These looked more familiar: a stickman-like figure in various poses: flexing muscles, lines coming from its eyes, stretched horizontally, shimmering, bloated . . . There were many and Toby had to scroll down the page to see them all.

'This is stupid,' said Emily. 'It's just another dull nerdy website filled with daft emojis.'

With a faint pop, a smaller window appeared on the screen. Paragraphs of text wavered between dozens of languages before finally solidifying into English.

'I can't read that. What's it say?' said Pete taking off his glasses and rubbing the dirty lenses vigorously on his shirt.

Toby read aloud, 'Welcome to Hero. As new visitors you have a free two-day trial download. Maximum of one download per person. Be sure to check out the mission board and don't forget to fight on for justice!'

Silence filled the room as they each took in the words.

'Junk,' said Lorna. 'I've heard about these things. They ask you to download what turns out to be a virus onto your computer then they take all your bank details.'

'It's called phishing,' said Pete.

Emily glanced at him. 'You would know that, wouldn't you?'

'I know a lot of stuff,' he snapped back defensively.

'So what's the harm? I don't have a bank account,' said Toby.

'Duh! Our parents do! It's all a big scam to get money!'

Toby looked thoughtfully at the screen. 'Maybe they're just games? And the first two days are free?'

'You're an idiot,' said Lorna.

Toby's cursor circled the screen, the pointer falling on the icon of the stickman crouching on all fours. 'We've got a virus checker. What's the worst thing that can happen?'

His finger clicked the button.

The screen seemed to ripple. Toby could have sworn the very material forming the screen bulged towards him like a funnel, whipping out to tap him gently on the forehead, all in a split second.

Lorna gaped at her brother, not quite believing her eyes. But the expressions that Pete and Emily wore confirmed that something bizarre had just occurred.

'Now that was a strange . . . optical illusion. Must have been. You OK, Tobe?' asked Pete.

Toby nodded. The room seemed to revolve unsteadily around him as though he'd been spinning on the spot. He placed both hands firmly on the desk to steady himself. 'I'm fine. Just a little dizzy.' The feeling passed as soon as he said it. He pulled his hands from the desk.

They wouldn't budge.

Toby frowned. He pulled harder. This time his hands peeled away like a suction cup on a window, complete with a loud noise like a Velcro-strip tearing. The others backed away from him, concern evident on their faces. Toby examined his hands. They seemed normal enough, if a little grubby.

'What's wrong?' asked Pete.

Toby remained silent. He stood up from his chair, hands held straight out with his palms up. His fingers tingled as if he'd been sleeping on them. Some inkling appeared at the back of his mind, spurred on by his overactive imagination.

'Something's different,' he mumbled.

Lorna raised her hand to his shoulder, but the expression on his face made her hesitate. 'What is it?'

Toby turned to the curtains and gingerly touched them with one hand. The material instantly stuck to his fingers like glue and would not drop away until he gave his fingers a sharp flick.

'What's on your hands?' Lorna asked.

'Some kind of electrostatic charge?' asked Pete. 'Like when paper sticks to a comb, or you rub a balloon on your hair and it sticks to the wall.'

Lorna shot Pete a scornful glance. 'Thanks for that, Professor. I am in the highest set for science, OK?'

Peter winced. He hated being called 'Professor', that was the nickname the bullies at school had attached to him.

A million thoughts swirled around in Toby's mind.

He'd read enough comics and watched enough hours of cartoons to be able to put the pieces together. Even if the pieces were extremely unlikely, or even impossible.

He turned to face a wall and extended his hands, palms up, fingers splayed. Toby licked his lips in anticipation; then thrust his hands forward.

They stuck to the wall!

Emily's mouth opened in amazement. 'What's happening to you?'

With a grunt Toby placed one foot against the wall, then the other. They stuck too. Whatever had happened to him had also affected the material of his trainers.

'What the heck?' exclaimed Lorna, astonished at the sight of her brother held fast against the wall.

'I'm walking . . . on . . . the wall!' said Toby in aston- ishment.

Using all his strength he managed to free his righthand and left foot, positioning them further up the wall.

Then he followed with his opposite limbs – pushing him higher up the surface.

Pete pushed his glasses firmly on his nose, as though it would dispel the illusion.

'That's utterly impossible!'

Pulling himself further up the wall, Toby positioned himself nose-to-nose with the ceiling.

'Impossible or not . . . he's doing it,' said Lorna in an awed voice. She was smart and, if she were under duress, she'd have to admit they all were, but Toby's actions defied both physics and logic, at least to the best of her knowledge.

Surely, she thought, if people could walk up walls then everybody would be doing it? She would have seen it on TV. A voice of reason chimed from the recesses of her mind: she must have fallen unconscious when the lightning struck. This *must* be a dream.

But as her nails dug into the palms of her clenched fists the pain assured her she was still conscious, which meant this had to be real.

'We'll be famous,' she murmured.

'That's awesome!' exclaimed Pete.

'No, that is so weird!' Emily added.

'Watch this then,' said Toby, now feeling a little more confident with his new-found skill.

Leaning backwards as much as he dared, he moved one hand to the ceiling, quickly followed by the other. Making the transition from vertical wall to upside down ceiling with his feet was easier than he'd anticipated.

'This is brilliant,' he exclaimed as he scuttled across the ceiling like a lizard, as the others started giggling despite their trepidation, 'except I can feel the blood rushing to my head.'

Lorna shook her head. 'This can't be possible.'

'You're right,' said Pete, grinning as he pushed himself into the leather chair and rolled forward to the keyboard. 'It's the website! It lets you do the impossible! Gives you the power. I have to try this!'

Emily craned over his shoulder. 'How? You can't just download it. It's not music you know! You can't download physical things. If you could, nobody would leave their homes! They'd be downloading pizza all the time.' She wavered, suddenly uncertain. 'Can you?'

Pete tapped the screen. 'Look! "Hero.com". Says it all. Toby's just turned himself into a superhero.'

Lorna tore her gaze away from her brother. 'Pete, no! You don't know the . . .'

Click! Again the screen seemed to funnel out and tap Pete on his forehead. He found the micro-experience unsettling. Emily blinked, missing the whole event.

Toby scuttled in a circle on the ceiling. He peered down at them, his voice filled with excitement. 'Well, what did you choose?'

Pete shook his head. 'I have no idea. I was going for the flying guy . . . but the mouse stuck. I clicked on something else.' He climbed from the chair and stretched his arms expectantly. Nothing happened.

'Come on!' he screamed. 'Go!'

'Maybe it only works the once?' Lorna said.

Pete walked around the desk to the centre of the room, where he stretched his arms out. 'The screen said a two-day trial,' he said. 'It's got to work!'

'Try and jump?' suggested Toby.

Pete jumped, his feet thumping hollowly on the floorboards. 'Nothing,' he reported. A sensation spread through his body, a pleasant kind of pins and needles.

'Maybe it made you stronger or something?' said Emily.

Pete flexed both his arms like a champion weightlifter as he strained what feeble muscles he had. His arms grew warmer as blood coursed to his biceps

WHUMP! Snarling orange flames covered his body as though somebody had covered him in petrol and lit a match. Emily screamed as waves of heat seared her face. She could feel her fringe burning. Lorna stepped back, too amazed to say anything.

Toby, who was directly above, had the full impact of the heat blast; flames singed his clothing. He threw his arms up to cover his face, flailed wildly and swung, upside down, from both feet.

Pete stood calmly in the centre of the room, staring at the flames dancing across body and clothing. 'I can't feel a thing!' he exclaimed. 'It tickles slightly, but it's not hot. Not even warm.'

Toby gawped. 'That's incredible.'

'It's impossible,' Lorna whispered. 'You should be burnt alive by now.'

Pete clapped his hands together - a blue spike of fire momentarily gushed from his palms like a Bunsen flame.

'Pete, stop it!' shouted Emily. She looked and sounded concerned.

Pete looked up with an expression usually reserved for Christmas Day. 'This is so cool! I mean hot!'

'You'll hurt yourself!' she warned.

'The rug!' shrieked Lorna.

All eyes were drawn to Pete's feet where a circular section of the fine-printed rug had already burned away, the edges smouldering in a slowly increasing circle. Toby just had time to take this in, when an ear-piercing screech made him look round.

'The smoke alarm!' he said.

'Pete!' warned Lorna. Then she saw something beyond him. Through the window, past the lightning-struck telegraph pole, a black BMW four-by-four had turned into the drive, windscreen wipers battling the rain.

'Mum's home!' wailed Lorna.

The moment Pete's attention faltered the flames extinguished in a dull thump. For a moment the four of them stood in confused shock, before Lorna gathered her wits.

'Tobe, turn the computer off! Pete, roll the rug up. We'll have to hide it for now. Em, help me stop the smoke alarm.'

Without question everybody moved into action. Toby scuttled down the wall head-first, and with a faint popping noise vaulted both feet off the wall to the floor and twisted his hands free.

Emily and Lorna dragged a chair into the hallway, directly beneath the smoke alarm. Lorna clambered onto the chair, which creaked under her weight, and stood on her toes - but still the button to mute the device was just out of reach.

Toby slid in front of the computer and grabbed the mouse, but he hesitated. If he closed the website now, would he ever find it again? Was this his only opportunity? This was something he simply couldn't ignore; the implications of what had happened were momentous, and he certainly couldn't let his mother's bad attitude stop them from exploring the find of the millennium.

Since turning twelve, Toby had never seemed able to get along with his mother. It wasn't as though he was always in trouble, in or out of school. It was just a feeling that nothing he did was good enough for her. She just always seemed to favour Lorna, and with his father rarely around, to whom could he turn for support?

His swell of rebellion was dampened by the sound of the car door closing. He knew he had little alternative. Thinking fast, his hand zipped the mouse pointer across the screen. Moments later the computer was shutting down. He turned the switch off at the mains: just his little contribution to using less energy and saving the planet. Then he raced over to Pete, who was struggling to roll the rug.

'Move it!' said Toby, helping him.

Lorna strained for the red smoke alarm button again,

annoyed at herself for not being taller. She made one big leap off the chair - and missed. Instead she landed on the floor with both feet, the impact causing a small table to wobble precariously.

'Toby!' yelled Lorna. 'I can't reach the alarm!'

Pete and Toby stashed the rug in a nook between two bookcases. Pete began to frantically stack the fallen books back on the shelf as Toby raced into the hallway.

'Let me try!' said Toby as he climbed on the chair.

But he was marginally shorter than his sister, and the button was well out of reach.

'Can't you climb up the wall?' suggested Emily.

Toby looked at her in surprise. Why hadn't he thought of that?

'Hurry!' urged Lorna.

Toby took a deep breath and launched himself off the chair. Pete ran into the hallway just in time to see Toby stick midway up the wall. He scrambled on to the ceiling as if it was the easiest thing in the world. Racing on all fours, he reached the alarm and stabbed the button - silencing it - just as a key was inserted in the front door lock.

Lorna used her foot to kick the chair against the wall.

Toby pulled his feet off the ceiling - and hung from his hands, unable to let go.

'Help!' he said, as the front door began to swing open.

Pete and Emily both jumped up and grabbed a leg each. Toby's arms and legs felt as if they were being plucked from their sockets as they tried to pull him away from the ceiling. He wouldn't budge. Toby yelled out in pain as Emily hung from his leg, her feet cycling wildly.

'Let go of me!'

Emily landed back on the floor. Toby heaved himself

back to the ceiling and flattened himself just as the door swung fully open. Sarah Wilkinson entered with her arms full of paperwork and her wet black hair plastered across her forehead.

'Hi, Mum!' said Lorna in a bright voice she hoped would hide her nervousness. Emily and Pete forced wide smiles on their faces and they all tried to avoid looking up at the ceiling.

Directly above them Toby held his breath, not daring to move a muscle. He didn't know if it was his imagination, but it felt as if his grip was giving way.

Sarah frowned, suspicious at being greeted in such a welcoming manner. She looked around. 'Where's your brother?'

'Oh . . . he's hanging about.' Lorna thought her mother looked tired; in fact she often did these days, and she hoped it was not because of her mother's diabetes. But even with the fatigue she showed, Sarah still seemed young for her age _ thirty-eight was ancient by any standards, and Lorna hoped that she'd inherited her mother's genes.

Sarah looked suspiciously at Pete. 'What's going on?'

'Nothing. Need a hand?' asked Pete, pointing to her bundle of papers.

That off-the-cuff offer of assistance deepened Sarah's suspicions. 'Seriously, what's happening here?'

Lorna smiled innocently. She was good at that. 'Nothing. We were all just . . . doing homework.'

A smell snagged Sarah's nostrils. 'Can I smell . . .

'Burning?' Lorna didn't hesitate. 'Yes, but it's OK. Lightning hit the telephone wire outside. It sparked a lot. Gave us all a scare. But we're fine. No damage done.'

Sarah closed the door behind her and nodded. She knew

her children's penchant for getting into mischief, but nothing seemed out of place. And if there was a crisis, she hoped she'd raised them to be self-sufficient enough to cope with it.

She was worried because they didn't see much of their parents these days. Her workload had increased, and her husband was forever away on field trips. Right now she was too tired, and wanted nothing more than to take her insulin and sink into a relaxing bath.

'If you say so. Just don't use the computer. I need to work on it tonight and I don't want it damaged by lightning.' Sarah moved into the lounge, her voice receding.

Toby let out a huge breath and scuttled safely down the wall. Lorna wheeled around on him with an accusing finger.

'See? You nearly got us into trouble. You and that stupid website.'

'What did I do?'

Lorna and Emily trudged upstairs. 'I guess that's the end of that!'

Toby and Pete exchanged a glance. They both knew she was wrong. Something like this could not be forgotten, or swept aside. Something like this needed to be explored and tested.

It was simply too much fun to ignore.

THE JOB_

Lorna heaved a cart top-heavy with local delivery boxes. Toby was with her, providing the legwork between the cart and the doorsteps. Following the previous day's excitement and resulting arguments, a sullen silence had hung over them. It was still there as they picked up their delivery round from the newsagent's.

For the last two years the local grocery shop had started home deliveries – local produce for the local area, and it had been a huge success. They had been amongst the first to take on the routes around the shop, while those adults lucky enough to drive did the further calls.

Their parents had insisted that earning their own money would be good for them. And, on the whole, both Lorna and Toby agreed – at least when Mr Patel finally got around to paying them. He was already two months behind, not because Mr Patel was mean, he was just forgetful.

Last night they had all gathered in Toby's bedroom before Emily and Pete had left, and tried to evoke Toby's powers again, after persuading Pete not to try his, as they didn't want to burn the house down. But nothing happened. Whatever magic had triggered the effect, it had gone.

After their friends had left, Lorna spent the night complaining that she and Emily had not had the chance to try the powers bestowed by the website.

Toby thought it was a typical change of attitude and had decided not to mention that he had saved the website in his 'Favourites'. He was still mulling over what had happened.

Overnight his entire outlook on life had changed. He'd always liked comic books and loved films, but he knew they were fiction - nothing more. The world was not under constant threat, people couldn't fire lasers from their eyes, and monsters were not real.

Yet now he'd seen the evidence of superpowers first-hand and if he was wrong about that, what else existed out there? Now the world seemed full of incredible opportunities. Suddenly it didn't seem all that bad. Perhaps that's why they didn't see their father? Maybe he wasn't a mild-mannered archaeologist but really a superhero, saving the world from heinous villains?

Stopping, he dutifully took the box from the top of the pile and approached the next house lost in thought. His hand reached for the gate latch, prompting the angry Rottweiler on the other side to bristle with fury and throw its full weight against the gate, which shook violently.

Startled, Toby backed away. The snarling beast clawed at the wire mesh, barking furiously. As gently as he could, Toby dropped the box over the gate, the confused mutt turning its attention to the plastic by trying to bite its way in.

Lorna snorted out a laugh. 'You're as white as a sheet!'

Toby treated her to an accusing glare. 'Oh, talking now, are we? Just takes my near death to get you speaking again?'

'Look who's talking! You haven't even mumbled for the last half hour. That's just not like you.'

'Well, doesn't this all seem, I don't know . . . mundane after last night?'

'How would I know? I never got to have a go.'

'Aw, don't start that again. You were telling me not to click on anything.'

'Well . . . I was wrong.' Toby blinked in surprise. Hearing his sister admit to being wrong was unnatural. 'And I wanted to try. Don't look at me like that. I couldn't exactly agree with you. Especially not in front of Em.'

Toby cast a last glance at the dog, which was now head-butting the container, before continuing up the street.

'Apology accepted.'

'It wasn't an apology."

Well, it should have been. What if I told you we could try again? Promise not to flip out?'

A smile played across Lorna's mouth. 'Really?'

Toby checked the next garden was free from predators before taking the next box from the cart. Lorna grabbed his arm before he could move away.

'Tell me!'

Toby tried to pull free, but Lorna wasn't letting go.

'OK . . . I'll tell you. But it's my find. My rules.' Lorna opened her mouth to object, -but was silenced by Toby's look. 'OK? So don't go snooping around without me. Do we have a deal?'

Lorna released his arm. 'OK! Your rules, I get it.'

'I saved it in the computer's *favourites*' Lorna looked at him in surprise. Of course, it was obvious! 'But there was no web address. Will that work?'

A shadow of doubt clouded Toby's face but he turned to

conceal it from his sister. 'Why wouldn't it? It worked well enough last night.'

'Can we try it? Later?'

'Well, it did say we have a two day trial. So it has got to be today. I'm going to call Pete over.'

'I'll tell Em.'

'If you must. So we're agreed? My find, my rules. Mum is out tonight so we've got as much time as we need.'

'OK. But this time we need to be prepared. I don't want us to burn the house down.'

'No problem. I'm in charge of the website and superpowers. You're in charge of safety.' Toby sniggered.

He'd just assigned himself the coolest job. Sometimes his sister was such a sucker.

The doorbell rang at 3:31.

Pete entered first, giddy with excitement and with a pile of comics tucked under his arm. Emily followed, shaking her head. 'He's been talking about Spider-Man and Superman all the way down here. *Incessantly.*'

Pete and Emily lived two streets apart, and their paths often crossed on the trek to the Wilkinsons'. It was an unavoidable fact they had both long come to terms with and eventually started to enjoy, although they would not dare admit that to anyone, let alone each other.

'This is all relevant,' said Pete. 'You're lucky I read these things, because that now makes me something of an expert.' The comics also proved a handy method of tuning out his parents' arguments, which had been increasing in intensity of late. Focusing on the world within a comic or a book allowed him to avoid the reality around him. But he didn't want to burden his friends with that.

Emily shook her head doubtfully. 'Yeah, right.'

Lorna led them into the study where Toby waited, impatiently pacing the room. True to his word he had not booted up the computer until everybody arrived.

Lorna nodded. 'OK, Tobe. Let's do this.'

Toby shot into the chair and thumbed the power button. He nervously drummed his fingers as the machine ground to life.

'I wonder if this will work without a storm?' he said.

'We better hope so. There's nothing we can do about that,' said Lorna.

'I haven't heard of anything like this,' said Pete, waving a dog-eared comic for emphasis. 'I searched online at home. Looked *everywhere*, but couldn't track that site down or find any mention of it at all. Nothing anywhere. No social media, blogs, nothing. It simply doesn't exist.'

Lorna snatched an Aquaman comic from Pete and took a seat next to her brother, as she flicked through it. 'So instead, you're using comic books for reference material?'

'Why not?'

'Duh! They're comic books. Not real life.'

'What if you're wrong?'

Lorna shrugged as though the answer was obvious. 'I don't think I am. It's such a geeky idea that it scares me.'

Toby stepped in to save his friend. 'Well they may not exactly be all true stories. But maybe they're written with some deeper meaning?'

'Like those fake news stories claiming Elvis lives on the moon?'

Emily frowned. 'Who's Elvis?'

Toby shook his head. 'So narrow-minded.'

Lorna thumped him on the shoulder, normally an action that preceded a ruckus chase around the house - but not this time. Toby was concentrating on the screen as the computer's desktop appeared.

'We're up and running.'

Pete and Emily crowded around him. Toby treated them all to an appropriately solemn look. 'Fingers crossed, everybody.'

He launched the browser and they waited for the homepage to appear. Electrons moved at the speed of light from their computer, tunnelling through the phone exchange and onward to their ISP server, located in a subterranean bunker somewhere on the other side of the country. The powerful computers relayed the information, identified the IP address of the specific server the home-page was located on and shot it back into the telephone exchange.

The data bumped a satellite ride, before beaming down to a receiver dish at a ground station. It navigated through the phone exchange once more, as it headed towards another server halfway around the world. The server acknowledged the request and issued a stream of data along a similar route - and back to Toby's computer, all in a couple of seconds.

'We're online.'

Toby moved to the *favourites* menu. He could have sworn the mouse pointer was moving sluggishly as he clicked. Another menu zipped down the screen, filled with a collection of sports and movies websites. And at the bottom: one simply labelled 'HERO'.

Click.

The page changed to a blank screen. Nothing happened.

Pete groaned in disappointment. 'The find of the millennium, and we've lost it!'

'Wait,' said Toby. 'Something's happening!'

The web address appeared on-screen, once more a moving string of illegible characters. And then the same basic page as last time appeared.

Lorna laughed aloud. 'It worked! Good thinking, Tobe.'

Even the excitement of finding the website took a fleeting back seat to the rare compliment from his sister. Lorna's hand suddenly lashed out, stopping him from enthusiastically clicking the mouse.

'Take it easy! This time, we'll read it, carefully.'

Calming himself, Toby clicked on the download page.

Again the screen changed to hundreds of separate icons; a pop-up window appeared, the text wavering through a series of languages before settling on English. Lorna read it aloud.

'Welcome to your final day of the free trial. Welcome, Heroes! Please choose your download carefully and enjoy an hour of super fun.'

Pete nodded sagely. 'An hour! That's why it didn't work again last night.'

Toby scrolled the message window down a little more as Lorna continued. 'Once you have chosen your powers, then please check out the job board.'

'Job board?' exclaimed Pete. 'Why would we want a job?'

'That's what it says. And there's a disclaimer at the bottom.' Lorna squinted as a slab of text appeared in a smaller font. She took a deep breath and read rapidly:

'Hero is not liable for any damage, destruction, loss of equipment, premises, or life; including loss of limb, brain function, or other biological necessities. Loss of personal possessions, sanity, or loved ones is the sole responsibility of the End User (He, She, It, who chooses to use such powers). We do not condone the use of powers for monetary gain, selfish or evil pursuit, and absolve ourselves from any such claim, misuse, or misunderstanding.'

'Wow,' said Emily. Her parents were both lawyers, so she had grown up amongst headache-inducing contracts and declarations that she had found around the house. Her father had even jokingly created one relating to dispensing her pocket money. 'Incomprehensible legalese' was the term he was most proud of using. 'Now *that's* a warning.'

'Loss of life . . .' said Toby quietly.

Lorna nudged him gently in the ribs. 'Not chickening out now, are you?'

'Well . . . no. Just . . . it didn't occur to me that it could actually be dangerous.'

'Dangerous? Pete almost burnt the house down!'

Pete nodded proudly. 'I nearly did.'

Toby shifted in his seat, suddenly aware that he was being the only rational person in a room of eager crazies. 'It's just that last night didn't feel dangerous. I mean, who created this website? There's no company name or contact information on it. Is this even legal?'

Lorna tugged the mouse from his grasp. 'Look, plastic bags have warnings on them, saying that they could be dangerous and cause suffocation. But do you feel frightened when you use one?'

'No, but I use plastic bags properly. I don't shove them over my head.'

'Then we'll use these powers properly,' Lorna said in a tone of voice that suggested further conversation would be pointless. She closed the warning box and was about to select a download option when another text-box appeared on-screen with a loud ping. She scanned the text with increasing excitement.

'It says: as a special offer, all powers come with a free flying upgrade to allow you to sample the jobs on offer!'

Pete and Emily erupted with simultaneous enthusiasm: 'Flying?'

The excitement was infectious, and Toby caught it again. 'OK. Let's do this.'

Lorna closed the box and hovered the mouse over a variety of icons.

'What do they all mean?'

Pete pointed to one icon that had wavy lines emanating from a stick figure's head.

'To me, this looks like some kind of vision power.'

'Vision power?' said Emily. She was feeling a little lost, as she hadn't read a comic book in her life and didn't really watch many films.

Toby waved his hand dismissively, as though the answer was obvious. 'The lines are around his head. X-ray vision, that kind of thing.'

Emily blushed. 'So you could see through clothes?'

Toby hesitated. That hadn't occurred to him; he was thinking more along the lines of walls and bank vaults. Seeing through clothing was another cool application.

Lorna pointed to a similar icon, but this time the lines were straight and dashed, not wavy. 'What's this one? Looks almost the same. Or this one over here?' In fact there were half a dozen icons, all subtly different.

Toby shrugged. 'You'll know when you try.'

'That's not very helpful.'

'Come on, hurry up!' said Pete impatiently.

Lorna circled the mouse, then clicked on her original choice, the figure sporting wavy lines around the head. The screen flickered, funnelling out slightly as though it was made from liquid metal. But this time it snaked at an angle - as Lorna was not directly in front of the screen - and poked her temple. She stepped away from the computer as she felt something course through her.

Toby looked at her curiously. 'How do you feel?'

'Can you see through my clothes?' asked Pete with a nervous tremor in his voice.

Lorna thought for a moment as she stretched her arms as though yawning. 'Tingling all over. What do you think will happen if I'

'Not in here,' Toby interrupted. 'Remember what Pete did to the rug? I'm sure Mum would throw us out of the house if you blew the study apart. Well, she'd throw me out at least. She thinks you can't do any wrong.'

Lorna ignored the last sentence, but had to agree with his logic. Trepidation made her voice quaver slightly. 'OK, we'll try outside. Hurry up and get yours.'

Toby nodded to Emily and gestured towards the computer. 'You haven't tried yet.'

Emily examined Lorna, as though double-checking that she were still alive. She scanned the icons, searching more for a pleasurable picture than trying to decipher their meaning. One depicted a figure with horizontal lines crossing the length of the body. This pleased her.

She clicked and the screen warped towards her like a living entity.

She backed away, shivering slightly as an agreeable tingle shot down her spine. Other than that, she seemed fine.

'Do you think it has worked?' she asked.

'We'll find out soon enough,' said Lorna. 'Somebody better keep an eye on the time. We only have an hour, remember.'

Pete pulled out his mobile and set a timer. 'The alarm will go after an hour.'

Toby was still feeling wary. He gestured to Pete. 'You're up.'

Pete eagerly grabbed the mouse. He hungrily studied the icons and chose one that depicted a figure with circles coming from his hands .'Let's see what this is.' Intrigued, he clicked and shut his eyes because the moving screen unnerved him. A second later a prickling feeling rushed through him from his head to his toes, followed by a warmth, similar to a hot bath.

Lorna looked impatiently out of the window, all too keen to step outside. 'Hurry, Tobe.'

Toby had had a little longer to take in the pictograms than the others. He slid the pointer across the screen and clicked quickly before anybody could see which one he'd chosen.

Click. Tingle. The gift was transferred.

Toby rose from the chair, a little unsteadily, and made towards the door. 'OK, let's try them out!'

'Wait,' said Lorna as she returned to the computer. 'Remember the instruction mentioned a job board?'

She scrutinized the screen and immediately identified an icon at the top: a rectangular frame with lots of small squares dotted around inside; it seemed an obvious icon for a notice-board. She clicked.

The screen went blank, and was then replaced by two buttons. One labelled: SEARCH BY DISTANCE; the other SEARCH BY RISK.

The second option alarmed her, and Pete must have thought the same. 'Click on the distance one,' he said. 'We don't want to have to go very far.'

Lorna complied. A list appeared on-screen, a heading read: NEAREST TO FURTHEST - 10/134

That's a lot of crime,' said Pete.

The first one grabbed their attention: CITY CENTRE BANK ROBBERY.

'What do you think?' Lorna asked.

Emily shrugged. 'Click it. I still think this must be some kind of weird interactive game otherwise we would have heard about it on the TV news.'

Lorna clicked before she remembered that none of them had watched TV that day, so had no idea what was happening beyond the back garden. A single word flickered up: ACCEPTED!'

Then, quite suddenly, they knew the location of the bank heist as if the information had been downloaded directly into their brains.

Pete spoke up first. 'The National Bank on the main street. I have a savings account there!'

Emily was surprised. 'How can we possibly know that?'

'Telepathy?' grinned Pete. 'This is getting cooler by the second.'

Lorna stood up, not thinking of the mission, but burning with curiosity about what power she had downloaded. 'Let's try them out, come on!'

Outside they stood in a line, all facing the giant oak at the bottom of the garden that had been struck by lightning. The ground was still soggy underfoot, but at least it was warmer out today. Toby glanced around to make sure there were no curious neighbours watching.

'Coast's clear.'

'I'll go first,' said Lorna. She looked at the tree and squinted, concentrating on making something transpire. 'Nothing's happening.'

'Give it a min' Toby was cut off as a brilliant flash of light burst like a firework from Lorna's eyes followed by an energy blast that struck the side of the tree. It tore a ten centimetre hole through the solid trunk and sent a shock through the boughs, shaking some of the tree's remaining brown leaves to the ground. Lorna was rocked backwards on her heels, and she fell hard on her backside. Emily and Toby, closest to Lorna, rushed to help her stand.

'Lorn, you OK?' asked Toby.

Lorna rubbed her eyes. She nodded, blinking rapidly. 'I'm fine . . . fine.'

'You hurt your eyes?' asked Emily.

'Don't think so. Do they look OK?'

Emily examined them. 'A little bloodshot, but nothing bad.'

'That was so cool!' screamed Pete who had been rooted to the spot the whole time. 'You've got laser-vision! That's unbelievably brilliant!'

Lorna composed herself, although her thoughts were a combination of terror and exhilaration. She looked down the garden at her handiwork. The hole was perfect, with the edges fused. 'This is bizarre,' she whispered under her breath.

Pete was almost bouncing on the spot. 'I've got to try next!' And without waiting for an answer he spun towards the tree and extended his hands in the best comic book action stance he could muster.

A stream of white liquid shot from the pores on his palms and whatever it struck suddenly had a coating of thick ice. Already he had sprayed enough to cover a two metre section of the tree trunk before he managed to stop the ice-blast by shaking his hands as though they were wet.

He whooped with delight. The layer of ice creaked ominously, but had already started to melt.

Lorna was caught in the extraordinary moment; the logical part of her brain was gagged into silence. 'Ice. Neat. That literally is cool. Em?'

Everybody turned to Emily who seemed to shrink back from the sudden peer pressure. 'I'm not sure I want to . . .'

'You'll be fine,' Lorna said soothingly. She put a reassuring hand on her shoulder. 'Don't worry about it, you'll be fine. I am, and Pete is, and he's tried this thing out twice. Just point, and . . . think. It feels almost natural when it happens.'

'I don't know what I chose,' she protested.

'Neither did we,' said Pete. 'Just calm down and you'll feel it tingling in your body.'

And she did. It started in her solar plexus, pleasant butterflies that spread outwards across the length of her body until it reached the tips of her toes, the ends of each finger and the top of her head. She had the impression that the tingling was continuing to build into a pulse as though her body could not contain it and should let it burst out, like a dam breaking under the surge of a flood.

BAM! It sounded like a miniature thunderclap from where Emily was standing. *Was.* Everybody blinked, but it was clear she had vanished.

'Emily?' For a brief second Toby thought she had

exploded, but something on his peripheral vision caught his eye – it was Emily.

She glanced around in surprise. One moment she had been looking towards the tree, and now she was standing underneath the towering branches. Her hand reached out for the trunk to steady herself, her fingers touching the rime Pete had laid down. 'What happened?'

Pete was first to deduce her power. 'You teleported!'

'What?'

'You've got the ability to move through space. From one location to another! Over great distances, or through walls! Well, probably through walls. That's what they can do in comic books.'

Lorna whooped with delight. 'Incredible! Try it again!'

Emily shook her head and walked towards them on her trusty legs. 'I'd rather not, yet. That's something I'll have to get used to.'

Toby flexed his fingers as the others turned to him.

'I can shoot lasers from my eyes, Emily can teleport, and Pete can shoot ice from his fingers. What can you offer to our little super-team?' said Lorna with a wry smile.

Toby licked his lips and remembered how he felt yesterday. 'I already know mine. I picked the same as yesterday.'

Pete pulled a face. 'Why?'

'Well, I . . .'

Lorna jabbed an accusing finger. 'You knew it was safe, didn't you?'

Toby stiffened defensively. 'I liked it. Didn't have time to explore what else I could do.'

'No! You used us as guinea-pigs just in case anything went wrong!'

'That's not true! I was just . . . I got scared!'

Emily tilted her head in agreement. 'Come on, Lorna. I don't blame him for that. I was scared.'

Lorna shot her brother a look that seemed to say 'traitor'.

Pete stepped between them. 'This isn't the time to fight. We've only got these powers for an hour.' He glanced at his watch, relieved to see that it hadn't iced over. 'And we've been out here about twelve minutes. We've got a job to do, remember?'

Toby blinked. 'The bank! In the excitement I'd forgotten about that.'

Pete pulled his mobile phone from his jeans' pocket. His fingers danced over the controls.

'What're you doing?' Emily asked.

'Setting the phone's alarm, so when it sounds we know our powers are just about to run out.'

Toby nodded. 'Good idea, but how are we going to make it into the city in time?'

Lorna held her arms out wide. 'Boy, you really have forgotten. We'll *fly*!'

Flying was not all it was cracked up to be. Pete, his head charged with the knowledge of a thousand comic books, had boldly strode forward and thrown himself in the air, arms outstretched - only to land face first in the mud, his glasses tumbling away, the frames twisted but luckily not broken.

After that everybody had been cautious, although fully aware of the minutes passing by. Lorna had criticized the lack of instructions that came with the powers and wanted to complain, but to whom, they had no idea.

Emily and Toby took a few turns, leaping from the wall that divided the patio from the shaggy grass lawn.

Neither had succeeded, although when Pete suggested they 'feel the tingle' as he now called it, Emily had dematerialized in a loud clap, only to reappear at the bottom of the driveway, a feat that once more unnerved her.

Lorna was the one to crack the secret on her first try, much to Toby's annoyance. She threw herself forward as though she was a goalkeeper diving to save the crucial World Cup penalty. As she arced centimetres from the ground her whole body slid forwards on an unseen cushion of air, and she gracefully pirouetted upright.

She accelerated to the height of the house, before slowly lowering herself back to the ground, whooping and giggling all the way.

'How . . . ?'

Pete began, still rubbing his grazed arm.

'It's so easy!' Lorna declared. 'All you have to do is fall up!'

Stony silence greeted this comment. Lorna's expression dropped as she saw the uncomprehending faces.

'You're a genius,' said Pete sarcastically.

'I know, it sounds stupid. But it's not. You know when you fall, you get that feeling of being out of control, like the ground has just slipped from under your feet and you reach out for anything to support you? When you get that feeling of being totally out of control, all you have to do is try and push upwards. Normally impossible. But in this case . . .'

She demonstrated again. The second time she displayed more grace in the launch and even managed to hover so she could watch the others.

'It feels like the most natural thing in the world, just like walking!'

Toby tried and failed, but at least he managed to land on

his side to cushion the blow. Lorna chided him, saying he wasn't trying hard enough.

Pete, glasses twisted back on his nose, threw himself with wild abandon - and swooped high in the air, much further than Lorna had dared. He even performed a backward loop before rushing head-first back to earth, only spinning his feet the right way round at the very last moment, before slowing to a perfect hovering stop next to Lorna.

'Brilliant!' he whooped.

Gritting his teeth and determined not to be out-done, Toby launched forward and lifted from the ground. His delight was suddenly tempered by the fact he was gaining no height and rushing straight for the tree. He heard everybody yell advice, but the words were gibberish to him. By sheer willpower, he managed to turn his body skywards - but not before skimming through the edge of the tree's branches, which whipped hard against his face. Once airborne though, he quickly worked things out and hovering soon became second nature.

Emily succeeded with her next attempt, although she zoomed around the garden like a rapidly deflating balloon before she managed to stop.

Once they were all airborne it was Pete's idea to head for the clouds and use them as cover. Everybody followed since they couldn't think of an excuse to use if the neighbours saw them performing the impossible.

Pete spotted the railway line below and followed it towards the town centre. He had always loved making maps, and spent a silly amount of time of randomly scrolling through satellite maps of the world when he was online. It was much more fun than then being cyberbullied on social media.

Next to him, Toby spotted the town hall and pointed it out. He opened his mouth to speak, but a rush of air swept the sentence away. He barely heard Pete's excited screams, as he wildly pointed towards the ground. But their meaning was clear enough. The bank was below them.

As they slowed to descend Toby had managed, at last, to speak. 'We can't just land in the middle of the street!'

'Why not?' asked Pete.

'Don't you think that'd be a little odd? There's people everywhere!'

Lorna nodded. 'Very good point. Over there, there's an alley. We can land there.'

'Yes, but same problem! Anybody in the street could look up and see us, even if we land somewhere out of the way.'

'Then we better do it quickly.'

'Anyway,' said Pete, 'who looks up in this city?'

After landing they stepped out into the street and headed towards the bank at the end of the road. The bank was old, with pillars holding up a porch on which was mounted an elegant clock.

Pete eagerly led the way but Toby caught up with him and tugged on his arm.

'We can't just go in there and start leaping about.'

'Why not?'

'Two reasons. One, people might recognize us. We should have worn disguises. That's why superheroes wear masks! And two, we downloaded the powers roughly half an hour ago.'

'More like forty-two minutes,' said Pete glancing at his watch.

'So unless the website can predict the future, we've probably missed the robbery altogether!'

'What do you suggest? We all just go home?' said Pete angrily.

Before Toby could reply a mighty boom rattled the street and he saw a black cloud billowing from the bank. They ran for cover as windows exploded in a shower of lethal shards, smoke rolling through.

Pedestrians in the street screamed and fled for safety.

The robbery was happening *right now!*

DOC TEMPEST_

Four silhouettes strode through the smoke, leaving the bank with an air of confidence, despite the chaos around them. Toby risked a glance from behind the bonnet of a Ford minivan that now had a football-sized lump of masonry poking through the windscreen. It had been the nearest place to hide. Everybody in the street had fled in panic, although the swirling smoke made it difficult to see very far.

'Look!' Toby whispered in awe.

The others peered cautiously from their refuge. As the smoke parted the figures resolved into muscular men, all wearing the same gunmetal grey and black jumpsuits, with a tornado motif on their chests. They surveyed the street, eyes protected by deep-red-tinged shades. Sleek combat rifles swept around the deserted street.

'They've got guns,' observed Pete. 'What do we do?'

In the rush to exercise their powers, the thought hadn't occurred to any of them that the bank thieves would be armed. Guns meant there was a very real danger of getting killed.

'Stay here!' said Emily. 'Let the police handle it.'

As if on cue the wailing sirens of a pair of police cars could be heard. The vehicles screeched around the corner, the drivers jamming on their brakes as they tried to avoid the lumps of concrete that now dotted the street.

The two cars slid sidelong, rubber from their tyres leaving black tracks on the road before they came to a halt.

The cops inside didn't even have a chance to leave the vehicles before the four thugs turned their weapons on them.

Toby blinked. Instead of the lethal hail of bullets he was expecting, the guns shot football-sized globs of black resin. The glue rapidly expanded as it came into contact with the police cars, swelling and effectively sealing the doors shut and blocking the windows. In seconds the two police cars were covered in masses of black glue. He felt Lorna grab his arm in a steel grip.

'Someone else is coming out!' she said.

Toby's attention was forced back to the bank. The newcomer was slightly taller than the gun-toting men. His head was deformed, shaped like a large drink cup from any fast-food joint, exposing a tall, broad forehead on which blue veins visibly writhed like worms under the milky-white skin. His cranium was crowned in lank black hair, which had streaks of white through it. He too wore the unusual red shades, and the same uniform as the others with the addition of a flowing cape that trailed on the floor behind him. Tight muscles flexed underneath the material, making him appear powerful and dangerous. In each black-gloved hand he clutched a metal, impact-resistant case. They looked heavy and Toby doubted all four of them together could lift them. Bundles of banknotes were trapped in the case lids, obviously having been quickly pushed in. His mouth was twisted into a playful grin.

'Bet he's the boss,' whispered Pete.

'What're we going to do?' asked Lorna, her voice tight with fear.

'The police can't even get near them.'

'We've got to stop him. That's why we're here, right?'

Emily shook her head. 'Pete, this is dangerous. I thought it'd be some kind of game or reality show or something!'

Pete freaked out, only just keeping his voice a harsh whisper. 'Game? Em, we just flew here. You're teleporting through the air and Lorna's firing laser beams from her eyes. How much more real do you think this is? Are you stupid?'

Emily was affront. 'No! I'm frightened! And we could die!'

'Come on. We're superheroes!' Pete was angry. Why had they gone through all of this, if not to confront the villain? Pete's daily life usually consisted of avoiding thugs at school, and the leg home was always perilous. He was clever, which made him a target. He'd long fantasized that he could have super-strength to pound his tormentors into pulp and now he had the means.

'Guys,' said Toby who was still watching the bank robbers. 'We'd better do something fast. I think they're getting ready to leave.'

The lead thug was staring into the sky expectantly. His accomplices had now formed a protective cordon around him, eyeing the streets for trouble.

Lorna took a deep breath to calm down and laid are assuring hand on Emily's arm. 'If we do this, we do it together. And if things go wrong, we leave in a hurry. Right?'

Toby's heart was pounding with excitement. Pete's eyes

were as wide as saucers; an expression Toby had last seen when they had ridden the country's tallest roller-coaster together. Emily was terrified, her forehead beaded with perspiration, but she nodded vigorously.

Highbrow tapped one of several buttons mounted on an oblong wrist pad strapped to his left forearm. He did a double take when he noticed the four kids walking bravely down the street. They spread out an arm's length from one another, and struggling shafts of sunlight that poked through the dust lent an ethereal effect to the scene. All that was missing was a theme tune and slow-motion walk. His henchmen whirled round, resin-rifles raised. But they faltered when they saw the defenceless children.

Toby could hardly hear his footsteps crunching the glass and brick debris underfoot and his heart was drumming so loudly that when he spoke his voice sounded distant.

'Robbery's over! Put the money down!' he heard himself shout.

The snarl that crossed the villain's face slowly transformed into a deep laugh that echoed spookily between the deserted buildings. He dropped the cases and pushed his hands together, offering them forward as though wanting to be handcuffed. When he spoke his voice was gravelly, sounding like that of an old chain-smoker.

'Oh, please don't kill me! Arrest me now! You're just too clever for me, kids!'

Toby and his gang stopped several metres away, the villain's actions catching them by surprise.

'Get your men to put their weapons down,' said Pete who watched them cautiously.

Highbrow scrutinized them like a headmaster over unruly pupils. He stood with his hands on his hips, and the cape chose that moment to billow impressively behind him in the breeze.

'And exactly who are you?' he enquired.

'We're superheroes. And we're stopping you,' said Pete boldly.

'Really? Superheroes, you say? Well, fancy that.

Impressive costumes. Part of the *Invisible Brigade?* Or maybe junior members of the *Titanic Team?* Well . . . people call me Doc Tempest.' He smirked, exposing yellowing teeth that resembled shark fangs. 'And I'm here to . . . *kill* you.'

With a casual gesture, his troopers fired in unison.

In times of danger the human body produces adrenalin to fuel an ancient 'fight or flight' instinct. For Toby, Lorna, Emily, and Pete the world seemed to slow to a crawl as the chemical globules fired from the weapons headed straight at them. They all chose the same initial instinct - flight.

Literally.

Toby, Pete, and Lorna darted skyward without thinking. Emily tensed, and abruptly disappeared with a thunderclap just as the glue-balls collided on the ground where they had once stood, and inflated into a giant gooey mass that would have ensnared and suffocated them.

Doc Tempest looked around in mute surprise. Lorna and Pete landed on separate sides of the street. Toby flew towards and over Doc Tempest, landing next to the large ornate clock that stood over the bank's entrance. He hung to the vertical surface like a spider.

Doc Tempest twisted around to follow his progress and was surprised to see Emily standing just behind him!

Emily was also startled to find she had accidentally tele-ported herself closer to the danger. She leapt into flight with her arms extended and swooped straight into Tempest's face. The impact caused him to reel backwards, and he tripped over the cash-laden cases and fell sprawling to the floor.

Two of the troopers reacted as Emily flew low across the street and fired their weapons. Tempest's men had endured months of hard training, and had already served in a variety of military units around the globe. Their experience had taught them to lead a moving target - so they fired just ahead of Emily's predicted trajectory so she could not outrace the gumballs.

Lorna reacted to the thug next to her just as he was about to squeeze the trigger. She squinted, and immediately a pulse of energy shot from her eyes and slammed hard into the man. He was flung five metres across the street, his gun melting as it took the brunt of the blast.

The front of his uniform burnt away in a large patch that revealed red scalded skin beneath. For a second Lorna was horrified that she might have killed him, but his groans of pain assured her he was still alive.

The other guy had fired. As the gumballs shot towards Emily, Pete extended his hands - a jet of super-frozen air leapt forth and shattered the glue-balls mid-flight. The gunman switched his aim to Pete. But after years of dealing with packs of bullies Pete had anticipated the move - and a huge ball of ice slammed into the man's face, knocking him unconscious.

Doc Tempest snarled with rage as he climbed back on his feet. 'What is this? Who are you little brats?'

Lorna stepped forward. 'Like we said. We're the heroes.'

'I have not heard of four . . . *children*,' the word dripped with sarcasm, 'that have proved themselves as heroes.'

One of the remaining two soldiers glanced at his fallen

colleagues in alarm and impulsively raised his weapon at Lorna. He barely had time to line the shot up before–

WHAM! Emily swooped in low. Having gained momentum by looping from the end of the street, she smashed into him like a cannonball. With the thug incapacitated she dropped to the ground, her feet sliding across the pavement before her momentum was lost; she felt like an ice-skater skidding to a halt.

Caught in the moment, she flicked her arms out as though she'd just finished a performance.

Doc Tempest growled, taking Emily's actions as a taunt. The remaining henchman backed closer to his master. Tempest took off his red shades and his bloodshot gaze bored into Emily. 'And what do they call you? *Zoom Girl?*'

Emily was repelled by his appearance, but remained silent, determined not to let the fear inside show through.

Doc Tempest looked up at Toby. 'And you, *Spiderboy*, how do you intend to stop me?'

That hadn't occurred to Toby, especially since his power seemed to be limited to climbing walls; not at all useful in a situation like this. He prayed that his thoughts didn't show on his face. Instead he shouted back, 'You've seen what we can do, so we'll just let the authorities take you in.'

'Yes, I have seen what you can do. Most unusual to have a new group of goodie-two-shoes just appear like that.' He snapped his fingers. 'Unannounced, with no publicity. But, my dear boy, you have not seen what I can do.' Doc Tempest extended his hands like a maestro at a concert; his voice suddenly raised an octave. 'A genius like me! And they send cops and children to stop me? Where are the Enforcers? Where are the real heroes? Do they cower in fear of Doc Tempest?'

Lorna had a suspicion he was being overly dramatic. Tempest slowly turned, taking in each of them. Then he raised his eyebrows and whooped with laughter as he brought his hands together in a powerful clap.

It was as if a nuclear bomb had detonated in the street. A shimmering wall of silver energy burst from Doc Tempest in a three hundred and sixty degree radius. Toby was the first to feel the force hit him like an explosion, sucking the breath from his lungs. The face of the clock next to him imploded in a shower of glass and ornate lead beading. He felt his body crush against the brickwork, his hands slipping until he lost his grip like an insect being blown from the wall. He fell.

Fortunately the bank's old entrance hall, which jutted a couple of metres below, broke Toby's fall. Slates cracked under his body and he slid down the steeply sloping roof, arms and legs scrambling, until he dropped two metres to the street below.

The last of Tempest's soldiers got the full blast of the force-wall, which sent him reeling flat onto his back and pushed him across the debris-littered road like a water-skier thrown from the rope. He collided forcefully with a Nissan car, crumpling the door with his head, and lay motionless.

Pete raised his hands to fire a blast of ice. He had no idea if it would work, but it was an instinctive reaction.

A jet of ice formed just as the invisible force struck - the sheer pressure curled the ice back against him, then shattered it into pieces. The cold ice fragments hit his face, smashing his glasses, as Tempest's energy blast pitched him hard into the side of a van causing it to rock on rusting suspension.

Lorna tried to leap skywards but the blast caught her and knocked her down the street, rolling her end-over end. She felt loose detritus, swept up by the force-wall, scratch her face.

Emily froze in panic, and suddenly teleported as the wall arrived. The energy blast dissipated against the clothing shop behind her, shattering the wide plate-glass windows into a million pieces, tearing the plastic mannequins apart with jagged shrapnel. She reappeared moments later, surprised with herself.

Doc Tempest looked equally astonished as he surveyed his handiwork and saw that Emily was still standing.

'You are a pesky thing, aren't you? But you can't stop me, little girl.' Emily noticed something in the sky above and gasped. Doc Tempest quickly followed her gaze, and smiled. 'Ah, it appears my lift is here. I'll have to cut our little party short.'

A disc shape descended from the sky; the gimbal mounted anti-gravity thrusters underneath hummed gently as the craft landed. At first Emily had thought it was some kind of flying saucer - right now, nothing would surprise her - but it was a circular platform, some three metres in diameter, with simple handrails around the edge: a *glyder-disc*. Doc Tempest seemed to control the final descent by adjusting a toggle on his wristband.

The skiff hovered centimetres from the ground and Tempest loaded the two cases on board, locking magnetically to the floor. The skiff swayed from the additional weight, especially when Tempest climbed aboard. He threw a little salute towards Emily and the skiff ascended with a soft hum.

'See you in the next life!' he warbled.

One of the injured mercenaries looked around. The henchmen's getaway van had been trashed when Pete was hurled into it. He bolted past Emily and leapt for the skiff. His fingers caught the edge.

'Wait for me, boss!'

The machine struggled to ascend any higher. Tempest looked down and saw his soldier hanging by one hand.

'Afraid not today, José,' Tempest purred and knelt down to grab the man's wrist. An icy chill rolled down the mercenary's arm. He howled in pain, but now could not let go as the frost slowly spread to consume him.

Toby groaned as he saw Tempest escaping over the buildings, the man dangling underneath was rapidly turning white.

'No! Don't let him get away!' he shouted.

Once the mercenary was frozen through, Tempest stamped hard on his fingers. They broke like glass and his body fell. He hit the ground behind several parked vehicles, but Emily and Toby both heard it smash. Emily looked away in distress. When she opened her eyes again she saw Tempest quickly disappearing over the rooftops.

Toby clambered unsteadily to his feet and approached her. 'Are you OK?'

'Yeah, but the others are hurt.'

They ran across to Pete who was on all fours, searching for his glasses. He had abrasions on his face, one nick above his eye bleeding badly from where his own ice blast had struck him.

'Pete!'

'I'm fine!' Pete waved away any assistance as he found his glasses. One lens was shattered, the other badly scratched. He put them on anyway. 'Where's Lorna? She got hit pretty bad.'

'I'm here,' she said.

Everybody spun to see her. Like Pete she had a few grazes on her face, and her black hair was full of dust and small pieces of concrete. Her face was pale, but she beamed with the thrill of it all.

'Now that was terrifying.

'Distant police sirens sounded.

'We better leave before any more police arrive. How are we going to explain this mess?' said Lorna.

Toby peered in the direction Tempest had flown. 'We've got to stop him.'

'Come on! He just batted us away like insects!' said Emily.

'We're still alive, aren't we?' Toby was surprised by his sudden conviction. The excitement had washed away the fear.

'That's a bonus!'

Pete took off his mangled glasses and examined them. 'My dad'll kill me for breaking another pair. They're expensive, you know.'

'We can do this!' said Toby enthusiastically. 'He caught us by surprise. We can stop him.'

Emily frowned. 'Why are you so eager to get him?'

'Because it's the right thing to do. We have been given a chance. A one in a million . . . billion . . . opportunity to do something extraordinary. To have a real adventure. We have been chosen to do this. I say we do it. What do you all think?'

Pete slid his scuffed glasses back on his nose, pulled himself proudly to his full height, and nodded in agreement. 'I say we fight.'

. . .

Pete had been right, few people ever looked up. As if they have a phobia of the void above, people rarely venture to look higher than eye level when they walk down the street. It was this fact that allowed Doc Tempest to fly through the sky undetected. Below him the few tall towers in the city began receding. Tempest was sure a businessman had been peering from his window, but knew that the man's brain would convince him he'd seen nothing more than a large bird swoop past. His skiff gained speed and altitude. The loss of his hired mercenaries was unfortunate.

He had a limited budget for hiring muscle, especially after blowing all his cash on his new secret base and the army he kept there. Running an evil empire was not too different from running any other business. It was that financial restriction that forced him to perform smaller robberies to finance his ultimate plan. Banks were never keen on giving loans to supervillains. Even though he would rather have worked alone, Tempest's scheme called for some additional protection while he amassed new funds. He knew the surviving men wouldn't talk when arrested. They knew better than that.

As usual, the authorities would describe the bank robbery as the work of just another organized gang trying to make a quick profit. Supervillains did not fit well in police reports or media broadcasts, even though they were involved in a majority of crimes. People would rather not think there were such things as villains with extraordinary powers and their own political and financial agendas. That would be too scary a concept for most of the population.

Tempest adjusted the speed of the skiff with a joystick on his wrist controls. He'd bought the control system from a secret supplier - a supplier called Basilisk.

The technology was well beyond what was readily available in most countries. The wristband controlled platform very much like a radio-controlled drone, and allowed him to keep tabs on his evil empire. And it was powered by his biometric pulses; again a technology that was far advanced.

Doc Tempest had had the unique ability, since his childhood accident, to manipulate the weather. His powers were limited to his immediate environment and he had been focusing his efforts on creating a super-weapon, something that could alter the global weather patterns on his whim. With such a devastating weapon he could hold governments to ransom. Tempest had a vision: the world at his feet, every citizen a minion or a slave, and the planet basking in a perpetual ice age. This was the paradise he saw every time he closed his eyes.

What Doc Tempest didn't see were four figures gliding low towards him. He wasn't aware of their presence until a heat-ray blasted the edge of the skiff. A chunk of metal was torn away, rocking the machine and forcing him to grip the handrail as his feet slipped on the bucking floor.

The four superheroes powered towards Doc Tempest, determination etched on their faces. Toby led the formation.

'Fire again!' he yelled.

But they had lost the element of surprise. Tempest banked the skiff down and to the right, forcing Lorna's second blast to miss. Pete was quicker off the mark and pushed himself into a dive, Toby and Emily following.

The buildings rushed up to greet them as Tempest raced between rows of tall tower blocks. They had travelled so far that they were over a different town now.

'How do we stop him?' yelled Toby.

'I'm going for the controls on his wrist!' screamed Pete

above the noise of the wind. He stretched a hand towards Tempest.

Something suddenly occurred to Toby. 'Pete! Your glasses! You can't see . . .'

With only one scarred lens to see through, Pete aimed at the blur that levelled in front of him. Power surged down his arm and manifested itself as a blast of super-frozen air.

The jet of ice shot wide hitting the window of the office block beyond, shattering several panes.

'I'll try again!' yelled Pete.

'No!' Emily and Toby simultaneously shouted back.

Doc Tempest raised his right arm towards the group.

Toby saw a flare of blue, and the heat of a lightning bolt singed the hair on his head as it passed by. Emily and Pete had to bank sharply away, and Toby lost track of them.

Tempest raised his arm again. Emily blinked – and in an instant she was standing on the platform, right in front of him. Tempest's head snapped round in surprise.

'What are you?' he cried in frustration.

Emily moved swiftly; her hand snapped out and caught the joystick toggle on his wristband before she suddenly teleported away with a bang.

Toby watched in awe as Emily momentarily appeared on the platform then teleported alongside him. But her job was done, the brief adjustment on Tempest's controls sent the glyder-disc into a wild spin. It barrel-rolled once in between two tall towers, before dipping across the roof of a shopping centre that was littered with outhouses, satellite dishes, and air-conditioning units.

Before Tempest could regain control, the lip of his platform tore into a metal air-conditioning unit.

With a crunch of rending steel the skiff flipped end-over-end, tearing up the bitumen roofing before coming to a sudden halt against the brick wall of a fire-stairwell.

Lorna caught up with her friends as they touched own lightly on the rooftop. The skiff made a crackling noise as something electrical shorted, streams of black smoke rose from tears in the machine's undercarriage. The two money-filled cases lay strewn aside, knocked free by the impact. There was no sign of Doc Tempest.

'Where'd he go?' Lorna asked.

Toby scanned the rooftop. The air-conditioning vents offered ample hiding places, but seemed too far for Tempest to have run without them noticing.

'Maybe he can turn invisible?' warned Pete.

'Great,' said Lorna. 'That's a nice thought. Everybody keep together.'

'Least he didn't get the money,' said Emily.

Pete knelt next to one of the cases and touched the tip of a note poking out. His mouth was dry. He'd never seen so much money in his life, and he wished every note of it belonged to him.

'How much do you think is in there?'

'Millions,' said a deep voice that made them all turn.

Doc Tempest stood on the edge of the roof. 'And we could share it all.'

For a moment Toby thought he saw a greedy glint in Pete's eye. He turned back to Doc Tempest. 'It's over, Tempest. It ends here.'

Tempest slowly shook his head, lightly touching the many bleeding cuts on his immense forehead, all sustained from the crash. 'No it's not. Not by a longshot.'

Lorna stepped menacingly forward, Pete following her. 'You're outnumbered, so give up.'

Toby was feeling a flush of confidence in anticipation of their victory. And at that moment Pete's mobile alarm suddenly beeped.

To Toby it sounded like the loudest sound in the world.

Their powers had just expired. They were now defenceless.

PETE SCRAMBLED for his phone to silence it, his hands shaking with dread at the knowledge they were all now defenceless and standing on a rooftop with a madman. Lorna faltered and backed away slightly.

But fortune was with them. Doc Tempest's attention was drawn to the sound of an approaching helicopter. Even from this distance Toby could see the distinctive blue and yellow markings of a police chopper.

Tempest snarled angrily and turned back to the group, stabbing a finger at them.

'The police have saved you this time! But mark these words; while you have ruined my plans today you have stopped nothing. With my Storm Engine I will control the *wever*! I will turn rainforests into frozen wastes, swell the oceans to flood the lands and ravage the world with ferocious hurricanes!' 'His voice rose to fever pitch. 'The *wever* will turn and my storms will force the world fall to its knees under my reign!'

Toby was uneasy, the conviction in Doc Tempest's words felt almost tangible, and a little funny.

Tempest flicked a glance at the approaching chopper, and then scowled the heroes. 'I will have revenge! You have not heard the last of me!'

Rocket pads on Tempest's boots suddenly erupted, and he was catapulted into the sky at such a velocity they heard a sonic boom seconds later.

Toby watched the approaching helicopter. 'We better get off this roof, unless somebody can think of a good excuse about how we got here with cases of stolen money!'

Pete stared longingly at the cases. 'Millions... just think about that. We could have *anything*. No more problems.'

Emily grabbed his arm, waking him from his reverie. 'Pete! We have to go!'

Pete reluctantly allowed himself to be guided across the rooftop. Lorna led the way to the stairwell Tempest's platform had crashed into. The smouldering glyder-disc blocked the green fire door.

'All together, let's roll this thing off.'

Even with their combined strength, it was a struggle. The machine rolled aside, just enough to allow Lorna to open the door. Inside a staircase offered an escape route down.

Pete cast one last glance at the mayhem they had left behind - and at the cases of money - before he followed his friends.

Without the benefit of superpowers it had taken ages to walk back home, and their feet were sore. The journey started with them excitedly replaying the events that had occurred - over and over, from each of their viewpoints. Toby's account of the events revolved around him as the central hero - a statement that developed into an argument between him and Pete. Pete accused Toby of choosing a power that was useless against Doc Tempest... and, of course, claimed it was *he* who had won the day.

Lorna and Emily had sense enough to keep out of that argument. They both knew it was *their* superior abilities that had defeated Tempest.

The argument had fizzled into an uncomfortable silence as Toby and Pete separated and headed for their respective homes. Before parting Lorna had made them all agree to get together tomorrow and try the website again. Pete and Toby merely swapped mute nods - both still fuming.

Pete and Emily walked in thoughtful silence most of the way. They were tired, their muscles aching with the kind of constant throbbing usually experienced after running laps in gym class.

They reached Emily's street, and Pete mumbled about seeing her tomorrow. He didn't hear her reply as he walked away - his mind was somewhere else.

He was thinking about the money in the case. He had never really been short of anything, although most of his possessions were usually bought in the sales or charity shops. He found it amusing that, out of his friends, he was the only one with a mobile phone. Admittedly it could barely make phone calls, and going online with it was impossible, but it felt a small victory. His parents worked exceptionally hard. In fact they were seldom ever together at home - something Pete put down as the cause of their continuous arguments when they were. If they were rich perhaps his parents wouldn't have to work so hard and then they would no longer fight?

Pete looked around. His feet had carried him to his own street, and into a gang of thugs.

He recognised them instantly: Jake Hunter's gang. There were three of them. Scuffer, Knuckles and Big Tony. All about a year older than him, dressed in torn jeans, dirty trainers and worn leather jackets.

'I'm tellin' ya,' said Scuffer in a low voice. 'I saw 'im fly. There's somethin' not right' He clammed up the moment he spotted Pete and watched him with narrow, rat-like eyes.

Knuckles took a long drag on an electronic cigarette that was cupped in his hand, trying not to cough from the alleged strawberry flavoured smoke, and then threw away the butt in disgust. Big Tony shoved a burger into his mouth, ketchup dribbling down his chin.

Pete's sore muscles tensed and his legs turned into jelly. He knew he'd have to run, and he was convinced his legs wouldn't carry him. How he longed for superpowers right now - then he'd put an end to the last two years of bullying he'd endured. He continued walking, careful not to make eye contact, waiting for the shouted insult or the sound of charging footsteps... but there was nothing.

He remembered Scuffer mentioning seeing somebody fly; perhaps he had witnessed them earlier?

'Hey, Professor!'

Pete's heart sank. Scuffer had detached from the group and was walking menacingly towards him. At least their ring-leader was missing: Jake Hunter, the one bully that no kid wanted to mess with.

Pete tensed himself and faced Scuffer. 'What?'

Scuffer was brought up short. Usually the Professor, like all of their victims never stayed around to chat, but today

Pete was staring straight at him. For once the bully was lost for words.

Pete experienced an unexpected a surge of confidence. 'I said, what? And the name's not Professor.'

Scuffer could never make eye contact at the best of times, and his eyes darted around. He took a step back. Pete straightened himself from the slouch he was accustomed to walking with, and broadened his chest as he shoved past.

Nothing further happened. Stunned, Pete cast a look behind. Sure enough, the gang were staring at him and mumbling between themselves. Something was clearly worrying them.

Pete smiled to himself. Could they sense the difference? He satisfied himself with the thought that If they *had* seen him fly then they could see he was a real hero now, and not somebody to be messed with.

There was no way Toby could sleep, not properly anyway. He was physically tired and as soon as he got home he jumped into bed, sinking into the blankets. But his mind refused to rest.

Tempest... flying... the resin-rifles and energy blasts... it was like something out of a game, but so real he could smell the flames caused by Lorna's laser vision and the thick smoke rolling from the bank. And something else, a sickly smell coming from Tempest, like he hadn't washed... well, *ever*.

Who was he? With a deformed head like that, Toby was certain he would have seen him on television before now. What could have happened to make somebody look like that?

Something else that bothered him too - his superpower had been useless. It annoyed him that Pete had been right about that. Of all the cool things he could have had... well, it was a lesson to choose wisely next time.

He flicked through the bundle of comics Pete had left behind and that his mother had dumped in his room. The immense possibilities were only just occurring to him. What they could achieve... what they could become...

Toby's stomach rumbled, and he realized that he couldn't remember when he last ate. His bedside clock said 9:30 p.m.

He crept downstairs, noticing his mother was on the computer, immersed in whatever work she was doing. He headed for the kitchen, but stopped as he passed the living room. Lorna was on the sofa, staring at the television.

'You're not tired either?' he asked.

Lorna looked at him with a grave expression and beckoned him over. 'It's too early. You better see this.'

Toby sat beside her. The television showed a dark street with flashing blue police lights and a presenter standing in the cold, clearly unhappy with her assignment. It was a discussion between the reporter and the news presenter, who was sitting in the warm studio.

'Police said it was an armed gang of at least five people,' said the reporter.

Now the images made sense to Toby - it was the bank they had been outside earlier. Toby opened his mouth to say something, but Lorna shushed him as she listened.

'And how much have the police recovered?' the studio anchorman asked.

'The police recovered all of the stolen money, estimated to worth in the region of five million.'

Toby sat up in his seat. 'Five million! Wow! What's that amount of money doing in a local bank?'

'I don't know. They never mentioned us though,' said Lorna.

'Isn't that a good thing? How would they explain a bunch of superheroes flying around?'

'They didn't even mention Doc Tempest. They said it was just a group of *ordinary* thieves.'

'I know it sounds crazy, but perhaps this kind of thing happens all the time? Maybe it's covered up, kept secret so people don't panic.'

Lorna nodded. 'Do you think so?'

'Somebody made that website. Those powers must come from some place, maybe even *someone*. And other people must be able to access the site too. So there must be other heroes out there.'

Lorna looked thoughtful, twirling a strand of her hair as she always did when thinking. 'Where do you think Hero.com comes from?'

In the comic books, groups of heroes were always banding together for the greater good, and he remembered that Tempest had asked if they were part of the Invisible Brigade. 'What if a group of superheroes had got together to share their skills?'

'Why would they do that?'

'I don't know. For the greater good?'

'Or maybe they're all too old to run around and they just want to retire?'

'Yeah, or they discovered there were too many villains for them to fight alone.' He stopped. The thought of there being other villains troubled him. Lorna was thinking along the same lines.

'Remember all those jobs on the website?' she said with concern. 'There was an awful lot.'

'And we stopped one of them. We did real good, Lorn. It's something we should do again.'

Lorna nodded, once more thoughtful. 'You realize that with these powers... we could be famous.'

Toby noticed the new copy of a celebrity gossip magazine next to her. She was becoming addicted to reading them once their mother had finished flicking through.

'I don't think that's such a good idea,' he cautioned. 'We can't run the risk of people knowing who we are.'

'Why? Think of the money we could make. The parties we'd go to,' said Lorna in a dreamy voice.

'We have to be careful,' said Toby. 'Imagine if somebody like Doc Tempest knew where we lived?'

Lorna shuddered. The glamorous life was suddenly forgotten as the danger became apparent. 'Then we're going to need something to hide our identities. Like the costumes in Pete's comics.'

'No! Absolutely not!' said Toby. This had been part of the angry conversation on the way home. Pete was enthusiastic about wearing a costume to hide their identity, and a 'Zorro' mask over their faces. But Toby thought that was stupid. He *hated* dressing up in fancy dress - there was no way he was going to wear a costume.

'I just think it's for the best,' Lorna murmured. 'Since your so against being famous.'

Toby stood as his stomach rumbled again, reminding him that he had been on a quest for food. 'Lorn, a caped costume is something that's not going to happen. My find remember? My rules. No way.'

He walked out of the room leaving Lorna biting her lip. For once she didn't want to argue with her brother. The scale of the superpowers made these arguments seem petty.

She looked at the clock and wondered when her mother would be off the computer, and preferably out of the house, so they could at least peek at the website one more time.

She crossed her fingers, hoping it would be very soon.

Slamming the mouse angrily against the desk, Pete shut down his arthritic computer. Since his return he had trawled the Internet in the hope that he would stumble over the Hero.com, but to no avail. He sighed heavily. He hated arguing with Toby, but he couldn't stop himself. To make him feel worse, he'd had nothing but a background sound-track of his parents arguing in the kitchen since he'd been home. It was always the same topic: bills and money. He glanced around the living room. It wasn't bad, but even he could tell it could do with some decent furniture and a new lick of paint.

The image of the cases filled with money drifted across his mind's eye. All that cash would surely solve his problems at home. It would certainly stop his parents arguing. Money solved everything. Or so he thought.

He wondered what spurred Doc Tempest on to become a villain. As he climbed the stairs to his bedroom, Pete could easily imagine his pockets overflowing with wads of banknotes. Was it really a bad thing to use superpowers to forge a better life for yourself?

But he knew the answer. Years of reading comic books had formed Pete's morals. Unfortunately he knew the differ-ence between right and wrong. Plus he had no doubts that using Hero.com powers to perform an unscrupulous act would get him banned from using the website. And that was too terrible to contemplate. He'd just have to make the most of the situation he'd been dealt.

He slammed his bedroom door shut to blot out his parents' voices. He was a hero, and he'd act like one no matter what.

Problem is, the villains always seemed to have the most fun.

A weekend wasted!

Pete and Emily had both visited Toby and Lorna in the hope that they would have another chance to try the website again. But that opportunity never came; Sarah seemed to be working on the computer all day, and had made no offer to leave them alone in the house.

Lorna had dropped a few hints to her mother, that perhaps she would enjoy going for a walk? This simply raised her suspicions, and Lorna gave up on that approach.

Toby started to worry that their mother had discovered their intentions, and was making sure the children didn't get to spend any time on the computer.

A phone call on Saturday evening drew Sarah away from the machine. The joy in her voice turned into melancholic tones as it appeared their dad wouldn't be coming home as planned, the dig was keeping him away for at least another week.

As Lorna and Toby listened from the top of the stairs, Toby began imagining his father with superpowers, travelling the world. He could only guess at the adventure he was embroiled in now. No doubt something big that keep him away from home for so long. Their mother's gentle sobbing brought him back to reality. He swapped glances with his sister, and Lorna walked down the stairs to console her mother. Toby would have liked to, but knew they would probably end up arguing.

Sunday dragged like only a Sunday can. Pete rang, and Toby let Lorna to talk to him. The two friends hadn't spoken properly since the mission, and neither seemed willing to make a simple apology.

It was clear their next dot-com adventure would have to wait. And with a sense of utter despair, Toby realized tomorrow was back to school - their half-term break was over.

Back to school... could that sentence sound any more agonizing?

Pete's shoulder hurt as he was slammed against the wall for the third time. His backpack slipped, schoolbooks tumbling into the puddles. He had attempted to repair his glasses with glue, but had ended up making then wonkier and now they had glue-prints over the arms too. His only other option would have been a pair of thick, cheap spectacles he'd been given for free by the optician. He'd thought that wearing those would make him more of a magnet for bullies.

Now as he looked up at the hulking figures of Scuffer, Knuckles and Big Tony surrounding him, he realized that his glasses didn't make any difference. He realized too that standing up to Scuffer the other day hadn't changed anything. The bully might have been distracted then, but today it was business as usual.

'Mornin' Professor,' growled Scuffer as he pinned Pete against the wall. 'Bet you were dying to come back to school?'

Big Tony sniggered. 'Yeah, you cry when it's the holidays, don't ya?' His voice changed into a high-pitched mockery of

Pete: 'Oh, no... weeks away from class! How will I learn? I'm so sad.'

'Leave me alone!' whimpered Pete.

'Or what?'

'You'll see!'

The response didn't sound like the threat that he'd hoped it would. The bullies jeered at him.

'Careful, Scuff,' grunted Knuckles. 'He's a black-belt in origami!'

'Think we won't bother you 'cause we let you go last time? Well we had bigger things to think about than a bug like you!'

A familiar voice suddenly called out. 'Let him go, doofus!'

They turned to see Toby. The hood of his coat was up giving him the vague air of a superhero and for a second Pete thought Toby must have been on the website to download some powers - he'd never stood up to these bullies before.

Scuffer didn't release his grip on Pete. Instead, wicked grins spread across the faces of the gang as they detected new prey.

'Or what?' said Knuckles, cracking his own knuckles - a trademark he had developed to distract from his reedy voice. 'What could you possibly do to us?'

Toby stood his ground, but he felt his legs tremble. The rain was pouring down, and it seeped through his coat. Knuckles and Big Tony stepped forward menacingly. Scuffer made no attempt to release Pete.

Toby stood firm. 'Let. Him. Go.'

Scuffer hesitated. His eye caught movement across the schoolyard.

'Here's the Man,' said Scuffer.

They beckoned to the leader of their pack. Jake Hunter was easily identified because of his shock of spiky blonde hair. Lorna had once mentioned that she thought he looked cute, a comment that annoyed Toby. He was a callous thug, and had no right to be 'cute'.

'Yo! Hunter!' Scuffer shouted. The grin that crossed his face dropped when Hunter threw a half-hearted wave and continued on his course - ignoring his crew.

'Told ya he was actin' weird,' mutter Scuffer to his mates.

'Fallen out of favour?' Toby goaded.

Scuffer snarled at him. 'Shut it. Must be somethin' on his mind. Come on, lads. Let the geeks go.'

He released Pete, and the gang followed Scuffer across the yard - all of them ignoring Toby. Toby sagged with relief; thankful they hadn't tried to pick a fight. He crossed over to Pete and helped him pick his books up.

'Thanks,' said Pete, feeling a little embarrassed.

'What are friends for?' said Toby with a half-smile.

Pete grinned. As usual their argument was now officially a thing of the past. 'Are you, er, you know...?' He looked around to make sure nobody was in earshot. Scuffer and his imbecile friends had disappeared around a corner. 'Powered up?'

Toby shook his head. 'No. But I couldn't let them do that to you, could I? We're a superhero team, remember?'

'I don't feel like one right now,' said Pete as he fastened the straps on his bag. Something occurred to him. 'What would you have done if they started a fight?'

'I probably would have been discussing hospital food with you!'

. . .

Torrential rain at break time had forced everybody inside, and with nothing much to do, a crazy sounding story soon spread that Jake Hunter had miraculously dragged a teacher out of a burning classroom on the last day before the holidays.

Toby whispered to Pete that, if it was true, perhaps Hunter had been downloading the superpowers too? Pete didn't relish that thought, and brushed it aside. He very much doubted Hunter would have done anything so heroic as rescuing a teacher. He probably started it. But the story was fast becoming a school legend and the shell of the woodwork classroom was evidence that something disastrous had happened.

The final bell sounded like an angel singing. Toby and Pete ran from the school into the heavy downpour outside, simply glad to be free.

Walking back home, Toby suggested that Pete should come with him to see if the coast was clear so they could try and visit the website. Their first steps away from school were filled with trepidation, worried that they might run into Hunter's gang. After a kilometre of peering over their shoulder, they finally stopped looking and Pete started talking about the website.

'Where do you think that website comes from?' he asked.

'I don't know. Lorna and I were wondering about that.'

'Somebody had to make it and put the superpowers on.'

'Yeah... so they must have had them in the first place if they're giving them away.'

Pete nodded; that made sense. 'How many powers do you reckon there are?'

'I saw at least twenty on there. And we didn't really scroll down the page.'

'That's mind-bending.' He noticed Toby was staring at the ground, with a troubled expression. 'What's up?'

'I was just thinking about Doc Tempest.'

'Yeah, that head! Maybe he has a disease or something? I hope it's not contagious. Glasses are bad enough, but I'd never make it through school with a head like that.'

'He said something about revenge. What do you think he meant by that?'

Pete waved his hand dismissively. 'Don't worry about it. He was just mouthing off. People say anything when they're angry. Look at my parents.'

They were several streets away from Toby's house when it became apparent that Lorna and Emily had also had the same idea about checking the website. They were just ahead, heads bowed against the rain and sharing a vivid red umbrella.

'Hey guys, wait up!'

Pete overheard them finishing a conversation about boys. Emily flashed a smile at Pete but didn't say anything. Pete glanced quickly away; thankful Toby hadn't noticed his cheeks blushing.

'You think mum won't be home?' asked Toby.

'You think that too,' Lorna replied knowingly. 'She's working at home today but was complaining that she had to go to the shops on top of everything else. And shopping takes her ages. I just hope we can try it out.'

'What's that?' Emily suddenly asked. She was staring ahead, over the rooftops. Toby and Pete followed her gaze. Pete swapped a look with Toby and circled his finger around his ear, a signal that she was crazy.

'They're clouds, Em.'

Emily tutted and grabbed Pete's jaw with her hand, angling his to face to the sky once more.

'No, you idiot - *that*!'

They all noticed it at the same time. A swirling cone of dark candyfloss cloud was forming a funnel in the sky. The tip of the funnel twitched like a cat's tail before making contact with the ground beyond the line of houses. As soon as it touched land, the cloud funnel grew denser as the twister increased ferocity.

'A tornado!' cried Toby.

Now they could hear the tornado rumble, like a deep jet engine. Debris spiralled into the tornado as they were sucked from the ground.

'But we don't get tornadoes *here*,' said Pete, not tearing his gaze away from the awesome force of nature. 'Bet it's about half a mile away. It must be ripping up everything in its path!'

Lorna suddenly ran forwards - as the tornado swayed drunkenly to one side. Toby shouted after her.

'Lorn?'

She stopped and spun around, tears in her eyes. 'Our house, Tobe! It's heading towards our house!'

Lorna fought for breath as they reached the top of her street. They all skidded to a halt to watch the monstrous spectacle. The tornado was the width of the road and moving at speed as it smashed through an empty house directly opposite their own. Windows shattered from the change of pressure within the building, and seconds later the front of the house exploded in a shower of masonry and wood. The twister ripped across the beautifully arranged garden, turning lawn into mud. The suction from the tornado was fierce, even pulling the rain towards it.

'Wow!' shouted Toby, both thrilled and terrified.

There was no doubt about it; the tornado was heading straight for their home. It struck a van, sucking it up like a toy as it dashed across the road towards his house - straight for the black BMW parked in the driveway.

'Oh God! Mum's home!' shrieked Lorna in a high-pitched scream that was clearly audible over the bass heavy roar of the tornado. They all took a few halting steps forward, then stopped. What could they do? Without superpowers they would be smashed like bugs.

Lorna felt Toby's hands grip her shoulder - they both watched as the tornado glanced the side of the BMW, tossing it away. It took half a second before they all realized the car was zooming in their direction, spinning like a coin.

'Run!' shouted Emily.

They scattered in four different directions as the 4x4 smashed down on the road, the roof crunching flat. The car skidded past them in a trail of sparks. But they were all drawn back to the tornado—

KER-SMASH! The tornado struck the front of the house like a sledgehammer. Roof slates shot in all directions, and somewhere in the chaos Toby swore he could see the front door fold in two.

The twister stopped moving, and spun on the spot, halfway in their home - but not advancing to demolish the rest. They heard a scream from inside the house.

It was their mother.

Toby sprinted forward, arms pumping. He didn't know

what he could possibly do, but knew he couldn't just stand and watch as his mother—

Once again he skidded to a halt - something was descending in the centre the tornado. The funnel was thick with swirling debris that made it difficult to see clearly, but the object resembled a circular metal platform... a familiar glyder-disc.

Toby was open-mouthed when he saw the distinctive figure standing on the platform - Doc Tempest! Inside the tornado the air was still and calm, so Tempest's cape hung limp. His face was a mask of delight and focused solely on Sarah Wilkinson, lying on the floor in the destroyed hallway of her house, her legs pinned by unrecognisable rubble.

Lorna, Pete and Emily caught up with Toby in time to see Tempest use one hand to push away the debris holding their mother - and then scoop her off the floor with the other. Sarah kicked and screamed as she was flung over his shoulder, and the platform began to rise back up the tornado funnel.

'MUM!!' shouted Toby.

He spurred forwards and was instantly struggling against the savage winds. Leaning forwards, almost at forty-five degrees, he pushed onwards. His fingers gripped a metal grill on the undercarriage of Tempest's disc-glyder and he was yanked from his feet, his body flailing wildly.

'Mum! Hold on! We'll save you!'

Tempest peered down, and snarled. 'This is what you get for meddling! She's my hostage now!'

'We've got no powers! Tempest'll kill him!' screamed Lorna. She ran for her brother, struggling free of Emily's attempts to hold her back. The wind slapped Lorna's face hard when she hit the tornado wall and her feet slid across the uneven ground.

Toby felt Lorna's hand grip his foot as he was pulled higher. His heart pounding, he glanced down to see Lorna precariously swinging beneath him. She opened her mouth to yell something - but didn't see a broken piece of furniture, caught in the tornado, whirl around and slam into her.

Toby stretched his free hand towards her. His fingers raked across her sleeve - but she lost her grip and was flung aside by the force of the tornado, as though shot from a sling. She flew across what was left of the office and smashed into the wall.

Toby secured his other hand on the glyder and looked defiantly at Tempest. 'Let her go!'

'You brats have ruined one set of plans! Now I've got some insurance that you don't do it again! If you do you'll never see her alive!' His peculiar, unrecognisable accent make the words even more threatening. Then something occurred to him. 'What's the matter? No superpowers? Ha! Then it's time to die!'

Tempest cackled as a stream of ice shot from his finger. It narrowly missed Toby's hand, but the cold seeping through the metal was so intense he felt his blood run cold; his fingers numbed and he was forced to let go.

Toby dropped, was yanked sideways by the whirlwind, and then hurled across the garden.

'Say goodbye to your mummy, little fake heroes!' roared Tempest. He was almost out of sight by now. 'And don't forget to clean your rooms!'

With a mighty blast of wind, the twister blew itself into nothingness - the sudden shift in pressure knocked Emily and Pete to the ground. A hail of rubble that had been caught in the tornado rained down, forcing them to shield their heads as it bounded around.

Emily was first on her feet and ran to Lorna who was slumped against the wall, groaning.

'Lorn, you okay?'

To Emily's relief Lorna's eyes flicked open and she nodded.

'Mum?'

Emily didn't know what to say. Her hesitation was enough for Lorna to understand.

Tempest had gone. And so had her mother.

Lorna looked around with a frown. 'And Toby?'

Emily pointed out of the destroyed house. Pete was leaning over the prone body of Toby. He gently shook his friend but there was no response.

AFTERMATH_

Lorna's own pain was forgotten as she knelt next to Toby. He had a cut on the side of his head that was bleeding freely. Trembling with fright, she stanched it with her sleeve as Emily felt for his pulse.

'It's strong,' said Emily. 'Roll him on his side, into the recovery position,' said Emily.

Lorna and Emily had both achieved certificates in first aid, but Lorna couldn't remember a single thing they had learnt. Emily was much more composed when under pressure, but she was still relieved when Toby coughed and his eyes flickered open.

'What...?' was all he managed before Lorna crushed him in a hug, squeezing the breath from him. Then Pete rapidly explained what had happened.

'You're a complete nutter, attacking Doc Tempest without any powers,' concluded Pete.

Toby didn't say a word. The shock at losing his mum had just hit him and he could find no words to express himself.

'What have we just done?' Lorna asked in a trembling voice. 'Where's he taken mum?'

Toby didn't know what to say. He and Lorna stared at the remains of their home. It reminded Lorna of a doll's house she had once had, one where the front hinged open, revealing the interior. Half the study and kitchen had been gouged away by the twister, including Toby's bedroom and the bathroom above. Papers fluttered everywhere as most of the books in the study had been torn apart under the fierce air pressure. Severed pipes shot pressurized jets of water out, while broken electrical cables snaked with a life of their own, sparking angrily. To top it off, Lorna swore she could smell gas; she was now worried the remains of the house would explode in an instant. The whole structure creaked ominously.

Toby's foot caught something. It was a small box that he instantly recognised. He carefully picked it up and opened it, making sure the contents didn't spill out and break on the floor. Several sealed vials of insulin and an injection kit. Lorna saw it, and if possible, became even graver.

'How long can she last without her medication?'

'What's it for?' asked Pete.

'Mum's got category one diabetes. She gets low on sugar and needs these injections regularly or she'll collapse. Even die.'

Toby closed the kit and held it tightly. The clock was ticking.

The fire brigade had arrived quickly and the children had been escorted from the scene by a fireman, who warned them that the building was close to collapse, and would probably have to be demolished.

Next, the ambulance crews arrived, and all four children found themselves draped in silver thermal-blankets. Paramedics tended to their wounds. Once the blood had been cleaned away they could see the cuts were minor, although the one on Toby's head looked impressive and needed a few butterfly stitches before a large plaster covered it.

Finally the police arrived, cordoning off the entire street since the twister had ravaged five other houses in its path of destruction. The police asked Toby and Lorna if the house had been empty.

They described how their mother was plucked away by the tornado - both children mutually agreeing not to mention Doc Tempest's involvement. After all, they had no idea if the police would believe them. Or who - if anybody - knew about these rampaging Supervillains?

The kind-faced policewoman who took their statement was surprised by just how well Lorna and Toby were taking the news about their missing mother. Toby overheard her talking to a colleague, asking for an aerial search for their mother's body; they believed she must have died. Tornadoes often drop objects miles from the point they were vacuumed up.

By six o'clock the police had to keep packs of news-hungry camera crews at the end of the street. They had no luck contacting Lorna and Toby's father, and their nearest relatives were in Australia somewhere.

Fortunately, Pete and Emily stepped in to prevent their friends from having to stay with Social Services. They said it would be okay if they stayed with them. Calls were exchanged, and with little choice, Toby went to stay with Pete, and Lorna with Emily.

Before they parted company, Toby and Lorna had a brief

quiet moment together - and Lorna went to pieces in floods of tears. Toby bit his lip to fight back the tears.

'You think... mum is...?' tears choked the rest of Lorna's sentence.

'Don't even think it,' he said sharply. He was feeling lousy and upset, but knew he had to be there as a support for his sister. He may have argued a lot with his mother lately, but the thought of her in any danger made him feel both angry and sad. 'Tempest *needs* her alive. I'm sure he'll have something to help her.' His voice broke, but he regained his composure. 'So you know mum's going to be fine. And *we* are the ones who are going to get her back.'

Lorna blew her nose noisily and rubbed her eyes. 'You mean that?'

'Completely. We're going to rescue mum, and put a stop to Doc Tempest.'

This drew a half smile from Lorna. Toby felt the conviction of the words burn into him, but he had no idea how they were going to achieve any of it.

Now Toby lay on an inflatable mattress on Pete's floor, wearing a pair of his friend's pyjamas. He glanced at the alarm clock, the red LCD numbers burning in the darkness. One thirty in the morning, and Toby didn't feel any trace of fatigue.

If only he had powers now, he'd find Tempest and make him pay...

Toby sat bolt upright, bobbing on the inflatable mattress like it was a waterbed. 'Pete?' he whispered. 'Are you awake?' Nothing. He tried again, louder this time: 'PETE! You awake?'

He heard snuffling from Pete's bed. 'Huh? Er, yeah... I am now. What's wrong?'

'We've got to go back to my house!'

Pete breathed out heavily. 'Toby, mate. You can't. They're probably knocking it down as we speak. Try to sleep, I'm sure they'll save as many things of yours as they can.'

'But the computer! It's the only way we can access the Hero website.'

Pete sat up in bed, instantly awake. In all of the chaos, he'd completely forgotten too. 'Maybe we can access it on mine?'

'How? We don't know he URL and you said yourself that your searched the net, but couldn't find anything about it.'

Pete nodded. 'You're right, we have to get to your computer.'

Then a dark thought suddenly crossed Toby's mind.

'If it hasn't been destroyed by the twister.'

Sneaking out of Pete's house had been simple, although they had run into the unexpected problem of creeping past Pete's dad who was sleeping on the couch, blanket drawn up to his chin and snoring loudly.

The rain had stopped, and now the town was shrouded in fog that gave the dark streets an eerie quality. As they approached Toby's street, they were glad they had it to shield them from the police officer sitting in his car, amid lines of 'POLICE - DO NOT ENTER' tape.

The cop looked up - and for one heart-sinking moment, Pete thought they had been seen. But the cop just glanced around, and then continued doing a crossword in his folded newspaper.

'Come on,' whispered Toby. He pointed to the nearest front garden. 'Cut through this way.'

He led the way across a driveway; both boys hunkered as low as possible. They scrambled under a hedge and into the next garden and continued down the street that way.

The gardens resembled disaster zones. Smashed roof slates, soggy papers, litter, splintered wood, glass, and - peculiarly - an assortment of socks. Toby didn't bother to check, but they were probably his.

As they had reached his house, Toby glanced back to see that the fog had obscured the police car. A framework had been erected across the front of the building, holding plastic sheets that gave the impression the house had been gift-wrapped. Toby found a slit between two of the sheets and they slid inside.

Pete flicked on his torch, which he'd thankfully remembered to bring along. It took several seconds for Toby to realize he was standing in what used to be the hallway. Looking into the kitchen he could see that the heavy oak table had been split in half, both halves then tossed against the wall, leaving huge indents in the plaster.

'What a mess,' muttered Toby.

He walked into the remains of the study. The damage looked particularly bad here, with a greater section of the house pulled away. Pete ran the torch beam across the room. Not a single piece of furniture had survived. The plastic sheeting formed one entire wall, while the rear window had been blown out across the back garden.

'I bet this is right where the tornado hit,' said Pete. 'It's a bit cleaner than the rest, like the twister vacuumed it all up.'

'Yeah, I bet mum was on the computer at the time, she

always is...' Toby faltered as he realized there was no sign of the computer. 'It's not here!'

Toby snatched the torch from Pete and started to kick over pieces of smashed wood lying on the floor. Then he spotted something, wedged under a desk-sized chunk with a light fitting jutting from the wood, giving testament to the fact it used to be part of the ceiling. Toby tried to remove it, plaster crumbling in his hand. It was heavy.

'Help me shift this!'

Pete found a handhold next to Toby, and together they levered the large chunk of flooring upright, letting it fall with a crash - revealing the battered desktop computer case underneath, the metal buckled and scratched and lying in a centimetre of rain water. The monitor lay next to it, tangled in a snarl of cables. The screen was smashed, and the plastic housing had cracked clean in two.

'I don't think that it's going to work,' said Pete.

'Oh, no...' groaned Toby as he knelt down to inspect the computer. A brick was poking out of the front panel where the DVD drive should have been. The whole case was tilted at an angle - *like the Leaning Tower of Pisa*, thought Pete.

'We've lost it. How're we going to get that website back?' said Toby with a hint of panic. 'How are we going to save my mum?'

His fist slammed the top of the computer, causing no damage what so ever; the machine had already taken enough.

An idea suddenly occurred to Pete. 'Just open it up.'

'What?'

'The casing, get it open! We only need the hard drive.'

Pete knelt down and began tracing his fingers along the back of the computer. He took the torch back from Toby and flashed it on a set of screws holding the side panels onto the case.

'We need to get these screws out. You got a screwdriver on you?'

'Of course I have,' replied Toby sarcastically.

Pete shone the torch around the room in the vain hope he could find one.

'Then we'll have to take the whole thing,' said Pete. 'Everything is stored on the hard drive. The operating system, your games, all of your parents' stuff and *all* of your Internet favourites. If it still works, all we have to do is take it out and try it on my computer!'

Hope flooded through Toby. 'Brilliant! Wait; if the police catch us carrying this through the streets at night, they'll think we nicked it!' He looked around the room, and had an idea. 'Pass me that brick!'

The policeman threw down the crossword in despair, and made another check around the street cordon. Nobody had been past for hours, and he was truly bored. With another five hours of his shift left he contemplated turning the heat on in the car again, but decided to warm himself up with a quick patrol of the area.

If anything the fog had thickened, and the officer tugged his jacket tighter to keep out the chill. He swung the flashlight around, satisfied to see the thick beam outlined by the fog. All the other homes had been evacuated because of fears of a gas leak, so the street was quiet.

Almost. A loud thump made the policeman stop in his tracks. There was another succession of loud bangs, like somebody trying to smash a door through. His hand withdrew his taser - a small stun gun that fired an electrical shock to disable any attacker. He'd been warned about possible looters, and the security of people's homes was in his hands.

His ears strained against the muffled silence offered by the fog - until he heard the thump again, this time accompanied by a metallic clank. *Maybe car thieves*, he thought.

The policeman advanced.

Toby withheld a cheer as the computer's side panel came away after he had pounded it with a brick. Unable to unscrew it, he and Pete had decided to use brute force on it. The open side now revealed the mangled computer interior.

Pete's fingers found the oblong black and silver hard drive half-hanging from its bay.

'This is it!' he said, as he pulled the cables from the back of the drive. It was a solid, heavy device, which he carefully passed to Toby.

'Will it work?' asked Toby, shaking it.

Pete's hands shot out, stopping him. 'Not if you keep doing that! They're sensitive devices, and after the computer was thrown around in that twister, it might be damaged. But it's the only chance we have.'

A blinding light suddenly fell across them. And with it, an angry sounding voice.

'You there! Hands up! You're under arrest!' shouted the cop, pushing halfway through a slit in the plastic sheeting.

Toby and Pete exchanged frightened glances. In a flash, Toby was on his feet.

'Run!' Toby yelled and powered down the corridor, shoving the hard drive into the safety of his jacket. He could hear Pete close behind.

'Stop or I'll shoot!' yelled the policeman behind them.

Toby powered up the staircase. From below they heard the sound of plastic sheeting being pulled aside with difficulty, hopefully slowing the cop. This was Toby's home, and he knew all the best hiding places.

'Why are we running?' asked Pete as he struggled to keep up. 'We're in *your* house, taking *your* computer! We haven't done anything wrong!'

Toby's voice dropped to a whisper as he reached his bedroom door.

'Because there will be too many awkward questions. Like why did we come back in the middle of the night to get this? We don't have time for complications, we have to find my mother *now*.'

From downstairs came the sound of pounding feet, and the crackle of a police radio. 'Sierra Oscar from Sierra Six. Suspects on Aylton Road. Assistance required. Over.'

Pete and Toby exchanged glances.

'Trust me,' whispered Toby. 'Nobody will find us in this house if I don't want them to. Now get in!'

He opened his bedroom door - and Pete's hands scrambled for the doorframe as his foot stepped out into the open air.

'Your room's not there!' screamed Pete. The twister had completely torn it away. They could hear the cop thudding up the staircase. They had no time left.

'Come on!' urged Toby.

Toby stepped out onto the framework that had been erected where his bedroom had once been. He beckoned for Pete to follow.

'We're superheroes, remember?'

'I'm off duty right now!' Pete retorted through gritted

teeth. But a noise behind him motivated him to move: the policeman was getting closer. He licked his lips and followed Toby, wrapping both arms around the scaffolding. Toby reached out and gently closed the door. The sound of footsteps suddenly came from just beyond the door.

'I know you're here! There's backup on the way and you've got nowhere to hide!'

Pete tightened his grip on the scaffold. He was feeling scared, after all he was up here without *any* superpowers.

A door slammed open from inside the house. It sounded like the door to Lorna's room. Toby nodded his head in the direction of the ground. Pete looked blank. Frustrated, Toby tried again, rolling his eyes downward. Pete shook his head, not comprehending.

Toby signed deeply. For a smart kid, Pete could be really stupid. 'Climb down! Before he opens this door!'

Checking his grip, Toby slid into a sitting position, one leg dangling over the scaffold. His searching foot found a cross spar, and it was a simple task to lower himself down to the next level.

'Just make sure you've got one hand firmly holding on!' he whispered as loud as he dared.

Pete nodded and copied the procedure. It was a little more difficult for him, being shorter than Toby, and at first he thought his foot would never connect with the scaffold below.

'You're doing great!' encouraged Toby.

Another door was roughly booted open inside the house: his parents' bedroom. His room was the next door along, and it wouldn't take a genius to realize they must have slipped outside.

Toby lowered himself, feeling the reassuring spar of the wooden frame beneath his foot as he eased his weight down.

But both his trainer sole and the spar was slick with rain. It was like stepping on ice. His foot slipped and he screamed as he dropped backwards, protecting his head from hitting the ground. Out of the corner of his eye he noticed his head was centimetres away from several rusty nails, protruding like claws. One head injury per day was enough.

Pete stared down, wide-eyed. 'Tobe!' he shouted.

The door above Pete opened and the cop almost stepped out, also forgetting half the house was missing. He steadied himself as he spotted Pete just below him.

'You! You're under arrest!'

'Jump!' shouted Toby. He kicked away the plank of wood sporting the nails.

Pete was alarmed as he looked between his friend and the cop who was holding onto the doorjamb with one hand and trying to bring his taser around with the other. It was too dark for him to make out they were just children. Pete jumped.

He crashed into the wood, remembering at the last moment to bend his legs and dropped into a roll to slow his momentum, just as he'd read somewhere. It worked, and Pete rolled between the sheets of plastic, springing to his feet like a seasoned gymnast.

Toby ran out after him, giggling with excitement.

'Pete, you were awesome!'

The complement washed over Pete as he tried to calm down. 'Got the hard drive?'

Toby patted his jacket. 'Right here. Let's go!'

They sprinted into the cloaking embrace of the fog as fast as they could. They had reached the end of the street before the cop had managed to retrace his steps and run out of the house.

In fact they didn't stop running until they were safely back inside Pete's. Wet, exhausted, and grinning triumphantly.

Pete found it almost impossible to wake up the next morning. But his parents were adamant he had to get up for school. Pete complained and sulked, but they didn't listen. Pete's mother had told Toby he could stay off school on compassionate leave, until the police could track down the whereabouts of his father. Toby had taken off the plaster covering the scar on his head, just to get a little more sympathy.

Pete was ushered from the house by his parents, who went their separate ways as soon as they reached the end of the path.

Toby retrieved the hard drive from his coat pocket. He knew Pete would return soon - they had arranged that he would skip school today. Pete would normally baulk at the idea, but he agreed that they were the only people who could save Sarah Wilkinson.

He dialled Emily's phone number. Emily answered almost immediately and put Lorna on.

'Hey Lorn,' said Toby. 'Emily off too?'

'Yeah, her dad said it would be better if I had company.'

Toby chuckled, that was so typical of Emily's parents. They always seemed so cool and accommodating. 'Pete's parents packed him away to school,' he said.

'That doesn't surprise me.'

'But he's bunking, and coming back soon.'

Lorna hesitated for a moment. 'Why?'

Despite the sadness he was feeling, Toby couldn't suppress the smug tone in his voice. 'Because last night we went back home and took the computer's hard drive. We should be able to access Hero.com.'

There was a faint gasp from down the phone. 'I... I thought we'd never be able to... I thought it would have been destroyed.'

'Hopefully not. You and Em get around here as fast as you can. We're got our own mission to do!'

It was ten thirty by the time everybody arrived. Toby had watched Pete surreptitiously walk past the house twice to double-check his parents hadn't returned home. When Emily and Lorna arrived, it was clear Lorna had slept very little. Her face was pale, and eyes bloodshot, but she put on a brave face and actually hugged her brother.

Pete rummaged through the utility room beyond the kitchen. In between the washing machine and an old exercise bike, he found his father's toolbox. He selected the correct screwdriver and held it aloft like a sword.

'Let's do this!' he said.

His computer was an old model, much older than Toby's and Lorna's. Pete unplugged it from the mains supply before trying anything. He slipped the screws from the side panel and opened it up. A cloud of dust greeted him, forcing him to sneeze.

'Are you sure you know what you're doing?' asked Emily.

'I was the one who last upgraded this computer.'

Toby looked doubtfully at the elderly system. 'Upgraded it from what? An abacus?'

Pete started to point at things inside the case. 'This is the hard drive. Looks exactly like your one. This cable leads to the motherboard, which is like the main part of the computer.'

'So we replace your hard drive with ours?' asked Lorna.

'That won't work. We need Windows to start up on my system; your version won't work on my motherboard. Wrong drivers and configuration.'

'You lost me,' said Lorna.

'Well, it *is* complicated,' said Pete, adopting the tone he remembered mechanics always used when his dad took the car in for repair. Emily snatched the hard drive from his hand.

'It's dead easy,' she said, rummaging for a cable in the recesses of the case.

'What're you doing?' said Pete, aghast as Emily pushed him aside.

'This ribbon cable connects Pete's hard drive to the computer. It has this other connection on it.' She showed them a plastic socket on the cable and slid it into the back of the new hard drive. 'See? Now your hard drive is piggy-backed to Pete's. The computer will see both!'

Pete watched her in amazement as she adjusted a jumper switch at the back of the drive, and then plugged a multi-coloured power lead into it. 'Just make sure the computer thinks it's a slave... bingo! Turn it on.'

Pete was open-mouthed, and for once speechless.

Toby burst into laughter. 'You should close your mouth. You're dribbling.'

Emily slid the side panel on, plugged in the computer and powered it up.

'How did you know all that?' Pete finally managed to ask as the computer bleeped to life. Emily smiled shyly.

Lorna shoved Pete playfully. 'Why wouldn't she know?'

Toby dragged up several seats so they could all see the screen. In moments the computer desktop appeared.

'This is it,' said Pete as he took the mouse. 'This is where we find out if your hard drive works or not. This is going to tell us if we can access the Hero website.'

He dragged the mouse pointer across the screen, and double-clicked his computer icon.

A STORM RISING_

LORNA AND TOBY'S MOTHER, Sarah Wilkinson, opened her eyes… and saw nothing but blackness. She wondered if this was part of a nightmare. She remembered working on the computer, and looking out of the window to see the clouds broiling in the sky. Then a whirlwind had stabbed down, smashing through the front of her house. After that, things got muddled. A distorted goblin face peered at her and there was the sensation of movement as she was hauled upward. She must be hallucinating and long overdue for one of her insulin shots. The sensation of movement was probably because she was feeling a little light-headed.

No, the movement was real. She was feeling it *now*, but instead of going upwards, her stomach was telling her she was descending at a rapid rate.

She couldn't move her hands; experimentation revealed she was bound at the wrists. A hollow metal clunking noise reverberated around her, and the movement abruptly stopped as she rocked to one side. Then a pneumatic hiss signalled the opening of a door in front of her. A horizontal strip of light appeared, getting larger as a ramp descended. It took a moment for her vision to adjust to the light, and when it did she saw two sleek rifle-barrels pointing at her. A pair of muscular men stared at her through red visors.

'Stand up,' one of them grunted.

Sarah took in their grey and black jumpsuits, and the curious tornado insignia on their chests.

'Nice uniform,' she said sarcastically.

One of the men simply pulled her upright, and shoved her down the ramp. Her legs felt a little wobbly, but her surroundings kept her mind away from feeling ill. She realized she was exiting the rear of an enormous Hercules aircraft, which was parked in the largest hangar she had ever seen.

The place was teeming with people, most of whom were unloading crates from the back of another Hercules. She looked at her captors quizzically.

'What's happening here? Where am I?'

The man snickered and theatrically gestured to the hangar. 'Welcome, you just won first class tickets to the end of the world as you know it!'

Sarah was pushed forwards at gunpoint. She took several halting steps - then a loud piercing alarm sounded, cherry-red strobe lights flickering on the walls.

'Look!' yelled her guard. Sarah followed to where he was pointing.

The entire hangar wall exploded in a bright orange fireball; the colossal power of the detonation knocked Sarah off her feet, sliding her along the floor until she crashed against the wall.

Gunfire crackled all around.

. . .

Toby watched the pointer on the screen turn into a spinning timer, signalling that there was nothing he could do but wait.

Then a window appeared... and a collective cheer went up as an icon for the extra hard drive appeared on screen.

'It's worked!' Pete grinned.

'Okay... let's see if we can get to Hero.com,' said Toby, pulling the mouse from Pete's grasp.

Toby connected to the Internet. He browsed through the Favourites list, which showed most of Pete's personal favourites, but with Toby's mixed in there too. Sure enough, HERO was at the bottom. With a shaking hand, Toby clicked, and whispered a silent prayer.

In a flash the screen changed, and Hero.com appeared with a message:

'WELCOME BACK YOUNG HEROES!'

Toby whooped with joy, punching a fist in the air. 'It works! Pete... you're a genius! We're on!' Emily coughed, and Toby glanced at her. 'Em... sorry. You're a genius too!'

'How does it know it's us?' asked Lorna.

'How does any of it work?' Toby replied.

'Who cares? Quick, get some powers!' said Pete.

'Wait a minute,' said Lorna, now standing behind them. 'We don't know where mum is. We just know Doc Tempest has her, so what's the point in getting powers just yet? All they'll do is run out. We need to find out where he is first then get powers that will help us.'

Pete bit his lip, and reluctantly nodded. 'Okay, but how?'

They thought for a moment. Emily pointed to the screen.

'The job board,' she said. 'Your mum's been kidnapped by a Supervillain. That has to be a job for a hero, right?'

Toby clicked his fingers. 'Brilliant.'

He zipped the mouse across the screen and clicked on

the pin board icon. As before the screen changed, shimmering through dozens of languages before settling onto English. Then, two familiar buttons:

'SEARCH BY DISTANCE' and 'SEARCH BY RISK'.

'Whose risk?' Pete muttered.

'Try the distance one,' said Lorna. 'This is where it happened.'

Toby selected and once more a huge list of bullet-pointed jobs appeared. They scanned through.

'Kidnap... kidnap...' recited Toby under his breath. 'Here!'

He selected: 'GALLERY OWNER KIDNAPPED'

'It's some Ukrainian guy. Wrong one.' Toby closed it, and felt a twinge of guilt. Someone, somewhere was out there, suffering. And they had just passed-up the opportunity to help. Then something else caught his eye.

'Another one,' he said, clicking on the option.

'WOMAN KIDNAPPED BY DOC TEMPEST'

Toby clicked the mouse. Another message appeared onscreen. Something they hadn't seen before:

'UNABLE TO SELECT: RESCUE MISSION IN PROGRESS.'

They all exchanged glances.

'What's that supposed to mean?' asked Pete.

'That means there are *other* superheroes out there,' said Lorna. 'Just like us!'

KER-BOOM! Sarah was knocked from her feet as a stack of crates exploded close by. They had been destroyed by a guy, dressed head-to-toe in blue, who was *flying* through the air firing energy-bolts from his fingertips.

Sarah gawped. That simply wasn't possible.

Another figure flew past and pirouetted skilfully in the air, before landing next to her. This one was a dark-skinned woman, who was maybe eighteen. She had her mobile phone strapped to her forearm, the screen glowing.

'Sarah Wilkinson?' the woman asked.

Sarah nodded weakly and thought must need her medication badly as the visions in front of her looked so real. 'How are you... flying?'

The girl managed as smile. 'We're the Titanic Team. We're superheroes and we're here to save you! Don't worry, I just—'

The woman jerked as a stream of glue-bullets slammed her hard into the fuselage of a Hercules. Sarah blinked; the woman was motionless.

Sarah turned around to see that the armed men who had held her prisoner had surrounded the blue-clad superhero - who was stuck to the ground, one foot in a ball of resin. A pair of resin blobs covered his hands preventing him from firing energy-bolts.

The soldiers parted as a pale muscular figure entered the hangar and strode towards the group, humming to himself. Sarah gasped; she'd remember the deformed head of her kidnapper anywhere.

Tempest stood in front of the terrified superhero, sizing him up.

'You won't get away with this Tempest!'

'Won't I?' said Tempest, and for a moment it looked like tears were welling. 'Boohoo, then I guess I should just let you go?'

The hero blinked, unsure what to say next. 'That would be a good idea.'

The tears evaporated like magic and Tempest pointed at Sarah. 'Trying to save her, eh? Problem is, now you found my crib I can't let you go telling all those other superheroes types can I? Bet it took a lot of detective work to get you here.'

Tempest strolled over to Sarah, skipping the last few steps. Sarah's expression revealed her thoughts. 'You're crazy.'

'Crazy? You think so?' said Tempest leaning close. 'Actually, I'm quite smart.' Then he snapped his gaze back on the stuck superhero.

'*Titanic Team*, eh? You remember what sank the Titanic?'

He drew his hands back, skittering his feet to a tune only he heard. The surrounding guards edged a few paces back.

'It hit an iceberg!'

WHAM! A jet of ice spewed from Tempest's hands. Within seconds the superhero was frozen in a block of ice. Tempest pirouetted around and slammed his hands together. A shockwave of energy rippled out and struck the frozen hero - obliterating him into tiny fragments.

Tempest wagged a finger at Sarah. 'Now just sit back and chill out. Take her away!'

Tempest walked away. A guard pushed Sarah towards a door as clean-up crews started dousing flames, peeled the superwoman from the aircraft, and cleared up the shattered remnants of the other frozen superhero.

'MISSION FAILED: HEROES TERMINATED.'

'Terminated?' said Emily. 'That doesn't sound good.'

'You think they died?' asked Pete with morbid curiosity.

Another message flashed up:

'DO YOU WISH TO ACCEPT THIS MISSION?'

Suddenly Pete was not so sure. He exchanged anxious glances with the others. 'What do you think? It... it doesn't sound too safe.'

Toby looked at him in surprise, this was a real role-reversal. Pete shifted uncomfortably. He had the familiar feeling of being bullied into a situation.

'I've got to think about me too,' he said in a whisper.

'Pete, this is about our mother,' said Lorna. 'If you don't want to help...' Her voice trailed off. She knew they needed the help, but was it fair dragging their friends into this potential deadly problem?

Emily scowled at him. 'Pete you are so selfish! How can you think like that?'

Pete's cheeks burnt. He knew she was right. He closed his eyes and summoned his courage. 'Okay. I'll help. We're in this together, right? Do it, Tobe.'

He glanced at Emily, but she pointedly ignored him.

Toby circled the mouse pointer around the 'YES/NO' option. His mind was already decided, but he waited for a nod of acknowledgement from Emily and Lorna before he clicked.

The screen changed again, this time to short punchy paragraphs. Lorna read through it aloud:

'Sarah Wilkinson has been kidnapped by Doc Tempest, and taken to his command centre. The location of this command post is currently unknown.'

'Unknown?' said Toby. 'What use is that? How can we find her?'

'Shush!' said Lorna. 'Listen: Heroes are advised that Doc Tempest has developed weather alteration technology and is planning to use it for blackmail.'

'Weather alteration?' echoed Pete.

'He mentioned something about that when he robbed the bank,' said Toby thoughtfully. 'And it explains to tornado. But what good is this? It doesn't tell us where he is! He could be anywhere in the country!'

'Anywhere in the world,' added Lorna.

Emily frowned. 'So where do we look? Or do we just sit here and wait?'

Everybody remained silent for several seconds. Lorna twirled her hair and squinted at the screen.

'Let's think about this logically. Whoever created the website must have had a reason to go to all of this effort.'

'That's right,' said Pete. 'For us to fight the bad guys.'

'But why?'

'Why? Because it's cool, that's why! Somewhere out there is a superhero with a bunch of powers he wants to share with the world.'

'Or it could be several people,' Toby mused. 'All sharing their powers with whoever wants to use them.'

Lorna began pacing the room. 'But why would they do that?'

Toby rolled his eyes. 'What does it matter?'

'If we work out the motives of whoever created Hero.-com, then we can start working out how to use this website properly and that way we might find mum. Everything on here is mostly an icon, with no indication as to what they represent. What does that tell us?'

'That they're trying to reach people across the world, regardless of language?' said Emily.

Pete stared at her with admiration. 'That was impressive. But you'd still have to be smart to work them all out.'

'Exactly!'

Pete blinked. He was getting lost. 'I don't follow.'

'Why doesn't that surprise me?' said Emily with sideglance. 'It's all a test!' She gently, but firmly, shoved Toby out of his seat and circled the mouse pointer over several mysterious icons at the top of the screen. 'They're trying to see if we're smart enough to make it as heroes.'

'Why would they do that, and who are *they*?'

Lorna hunched over the screen and perused the icons. "They' are whoever built this site. Look at the bottom here.' She scrolled all the way down the screen to where a small line read:

'Property of the Foundation,' she read. 'Obviously this Foundation must be superheroes, but are they retired? Are they so badly injured they can't continue fighting evil? That message said 'mission in progress' so we know there are other people out there, just like us.'

The answer hit Toby. 'We're being trained. As replacements?'

'Could be.' Lorna couldn't keep the tremor of excitement from her voice. 'This is all a trial, a very *real* trial, to see if we're worthy.'

'And what if we are?' asked Pete cautiously.

'Then maybe we get these powers full time?' She shot a glance at her brother. 'And maybe get to be famous from all this. Who knows?'

'Fame means money, right?' said Pete thoughtfully.

'Money's not everything,' said Toby.

Pete grunted and answered sharply back. 'Easy to say when you have it.'

'What's that supposed to mean?' Toby snapped back.

'I'm fed up with—'

'Will you both shut up?' shouted Emily. The boys immediately fell silent and looked at her in astonishment. They'd never seen the usually mild-mannered Emily get angry before.

'We're a team, so you better start acting like one.' She glared at them both for a moment, and then she broke into a pleasant smile and continued as normal. Pete glanced at Toby and raised an eyebrow - effortlessly communicating the fact that he wouldn't want to get on her bad side. 'It would be cool to track down the people behind Hero.com. Find out what is really going on.'

'But in the meantime, we have to get our mum. And *quickly*,' Toby reminded her. He tapped the small diabetes kit he now kept with him all the time. 'And I don't see how any of this helps.'

'It all helps,' said Emily shifting her attention back to the screen. 'It means that this website has some structure, like the job board. Which means there must be some blog or some way to share info. Ah-ha!'

Emily clicked one of the top icons - and everybody took a wary step away from the screen, just in case. The image changed to a rolling list of text entries, and a prominent 'search' box.

'Here we go,' said Emily with a broad grin. 'A blog. That icon looks like a finger hitting a key.' The others looked dubiously at it. 'Well it does if you looked hard enough.'

Pete patted Emily on the shoulder, as he read the entries. He didn't notice Emily nervously tense.

'Good thinking, Em,' said Pete. There were dozens of entries from an assortment of users with peculiar names: *Sergeant Power*, *Capman*, and *Thunder Girl*. And each had a few descriptive lines underneath that revealed a world of information - heroes spying on villains and reporting in on the latest evil team-ups, schemes, or their whereabouts. There was a *lot* going on in the world. Pete pointed at a blog halfway down the screen, leaving a greasy smudge. 'There! Click on it!'

Emily dutifully followed. It was an entry labelled: DOC TEMPEST from somebody called *Chameleon*. The blog unfolded into a short paragraph that Pete read out.

'Alerted by movement from Doc Tempest. Suspect involvement with the renegade Basilisk - sources indicate Tempest is selling him out to the COE. Tempest on the move for Council approval in one hour fifty-five minutes.' Pete pushed his glasses firmly up nose. 'What the heck does all that mean?'

'What's the Council?' asked Lorna. 'Or Basilisk?'

'They're code words, ' said Pete with sudden confidence. The others looked at him quizzically. 'Stands to reason if this Chameleon fellow won't use his real name, then he'll use codes for everything else.'

'Maybe,' said Emily. The time on the screen slowly counted down. She circled the mouse pointer around the bottom of the message. 'You missed this bit. Says 'click for map coordinates'.'

As she did a new window appeared showing the world from space. The globe swivelled around and zoomed towards an area of southwest France. Mountains, fields and cities became visible as the image continued magnifying until a small rural town filled the screen - a single field highlighted.

'Well, we know where Doc Tempest is going to be,' said Toby firmly. 'This time he won't escape.'

'Let's power-up,' said Pete eagerly rubbing his hands together.

The superpower page was different this time. A small

window had appeared, cascading into English to display a set of instructions. Lorna read through it:

'Now that you have been fully initiated into Hero.com your trial period is over. You have earned two HEROISM POINTS each, allowing the download of two powers per-hero for a maximum of 24 hours! Further powers may be purchased: Hero.com accepts Visa and MasterCard!'

'Purchased?' Toby shrieked.

'Knew it,' said Lorna triumphantly. 'Dad always says you get nothing for free!'

'What are you talking about?' said Pete. 'We each got heroism points for free!'

'That was for stopping Tempest's bank robbery,' Emily pointed out. 'Does that mean if we fail, we don't get any points?'

'Maybe it's like levels; the more heroic stuff you do, the more you get to download?'

'Excellent!' said Pete who hoped that tidying his room would earn him something, even if his parents never bothered to ask him to do it.

'We haven't got time to debate this,' said Lorna. 'We've got two powers and the clock is ticking!'

'At least we have these powers longer than an hour this time,' said Pete.

'I suggest we all choose flying as one,' said Lorna. 'We have to get there after all.'

'Okay, I'll go first,' said Emily. 'Er... which one is flying? We didn't have to choose it last time.'

'Remember, there *is* some logic to this site,' said Lorna.

Emily glided through the icons before settling on one they all agreed must be flying. Her finger hesitated over the mouse button. She turned to Toby. 'And this time, you better pick something useful!'

Then she clicked the mouse.

The flight was peaceful enough once they had lifted above the cloud cover. The blue skies beyond allowed the sun to pleasantly shine down on them.

Before they left, Pete had run off to change into a wetsuit he'd had when he was younger, and thus, smaller. The neoprene material was stretched to breaking point to cover him. He'd also found a cape from an old fancy dress costume and a pair of blue, prescription-swimming goggles he used as a mask. When he'd modelled his new superhero outfit to the others, they had wasted precious moments curled up giggling. He looked a complete idiot.

Now he was paying the price as the sun heated the suit so that he was sweating profusely. He'd already had to lose the cape, as the wind pulled it so tight it had nearly choked him, and his mask had slipped off too.

The team had overlooked one important factor. They had assumed that flying, they would be there in a jiffy. But that was in the movies. It turned out, even at full speed, which seemed as fast as a bullet to them, it had taken almost two hours to reach the field. At one point, they had to land to consult local signposts to ensure they were heading in the right direction. But at the very least, that had improved their landing and taking off skills.

They arrived at sunset. From the air they could see that the field was no longer empty - a large circular metallic building was sitting there. Confused, Toby checked a map they had printed from the web that showed the far off Pyrenees Mountains to the south and the layout of the village with its old church and crumbling chateau on a hill. They were in the right place.

The team landed on the edge of the village and kept concealed behind an old stonewall. They stealthily crossed the dusty road, ducking behind another wall just as a pair of Tempest's soldiers marched down the street. Their footsteps echoed from the buildings, and the heroes all held their breath as the men passed a metre away.

Toby indicated with swift hand gestures that they should head around the back of a barn and into a copse of ancient cedars. They kept low and silent as they ran. Old war movies came to Pete's mind as they slipped behind another pair of guards who were talking animatedly about sports cars.

Hiding in the trees, the children were now sheltered from being spotted by the squaddies.

Toby turned his attention to the building in the field, and gasped. From ground level it was obviously the structure was actually an aircraft of some kind, supported on six massive landing legs that pushed into the field. The diameter of the craft was three times as long as any jumbo jet Toby had seen.

'Wow!' whispered Pete. 'It's like a giant flying saucer!'

Gentle vents of steam rolled from outlets across the undercarriage. Two guards stood to attention at the bottom of a boarding ramp that vanished into the belly of the machine.

'I see only one way in,' said Emily.

'You think mum's in there?'

Toby shrugged. Then they heard a new voice.

'I'm afraid that she's not.'

Everybody spun around ready to unleash their super-powers. A young man with a pale face and jet-black hair, which was oddly laced with snow, was studying them carefully. He shook more snow off his long black trench coat, the warm French air soon melting it.

'Who are you?' Toby demanded.

'And why're you covered in snow?' asked Pete more than a little perplexed.

The stranger raised his hands in a friendly gesture. 'Relax, I'm with you. I'm known as Chameleon. And to answer your other question I've just teléported in from Russia. I assure you it's *very* cold there.'

They noticed scratches on his face and his nose seemed to be a little askew. With a jarring crack, Chameleon's nose realigned itself and his scars faded.

Toby was impressed. 'Wow, healing. That's a good power to have.'

'Unfortunately you still feel the pain. My apologies, I didn't mean to alarm you. But I was hit by a truck before I left.' He ignored their sceptical glances. 'Unless I'm very much mistaken, you came here because of Hero.com?'

Everybody relaxed, except Pete who eyed the stranger suspiciously. Chameleon approached them with a calculating look. 'I've been tracking a network of supervillains for some time. It appears Doc Tempest is involved with a breakaway faction of the Council of Evil. Specifically a devious villain named Basilisk who is upsetting a lot of people on both sides of the fence.' He indicated to the ship. 'That's why the Council has summoned Tempest here, to explain himself. He won't allow the Council of Evil direct communication to his base for fear they will try and shut down his operation. And they certainly don't want Tempest turning up at their headquarters. Wherever that is. That's something we'd love to discover.' He added dreamily.

Lorna glanced at the ship. She noticed that there was a

large triangular emblem on the side of the craft with a stylized letter 'C' in the middle. Chameleon detected his audience's confusion.

'You have not been doing this too long have you? Didn't you read the site's instructions file? I know it's a lengthy tome, but it's all there.'

'Instructions?' said Pete, finally letting his guard down.

Chameleon blinked in surprise, and he held back a laugh. 'Don't tell me you've been making it all up as you go? Surely not! It's labelled READ ME in big letters! That's a new one! Ha, ha...'

Pete looked abashed, but Lorna stepped forward. She felt angry that this new guy was mocking them.

'We've done pretty well on our own so far. So if you're just going to stand there and criticise then you can get lost! My mum's been taken by that freak and if he's in there, I want answers!'

Chameleon bowed slightly. 'I'm sorry. I didn't mean to offend. Well, not too much.' He studied the group as though reappraising them. 'And if you've fought Doc Tempest before and survived,' he noticed the fresh scar on Toby's head and tapped it with his finger. The scar healed, the stitches melting away leaving nothing but smooth skin. Chameleon continued, 'then you certainly are talented. If you want to question Tempest, then I suggest we board the ship and do it there.'

'Shouldn't we wait until he comes out?' asked Toby.

'His men are patrolling the area, but they are not allowed on the Council's ship. There is little security onboard since none of the Council of Evil is actually present. Plus they will want to get out of here as fast as possible because they know the Enforcers are heading this way now.'

'The Enforcers?' asked Toby.

'They're an elite group of soldiers. Created by the United Nation and trained to combat supervillains and rogue heroes. They have a wealth of technological gizmos at their disposal, but alas, none of them possess superpowers and have to resort to more conventional means of travel. Which is why they have not yet arrived. The Council chooses its landing places entirely at random, which also throws the Enforcer's off balance.'

'Why don't they just download the powers like we did?' asked Toby.

'The Enforcers are soldiers. Trained in killing. They're not the type of people you want downloading such powers willy-nilly. They've been following Tempest for the last year but his movements have been erratic, therefore unpredictable.'

'What is this Council?' Emily asked.

'The Council of Evil, it's all on the FAQ,' Chameleon replied, a little testily.

Lorna was about to ask what 'FAQ' meant, but Pete nudged her and whispered, 'Frequently Asked Questions.'

Pete and Lorna looked daunted, there was obviously more to this superhero venture than they'd suspected. As usually, Emily was a little quicker on the uptake.

'So the Council are a ruling group of villains?'

'Exactly. Some of the most twisted minds the world has ever seen.'

'Do you have a plan for getting in there?' asked Toby, returning his gaze to the huge ship.

'That's the easy part,' said Chameleon.

Chameleon's face began to change. The skin moved fluidly until his face resembled one of the guards, tinted-visor and all. Chameleon's entire body wavered as it morphed. His long black trench coat shrank and warped into the uniform of Tempest's guards. One of his hands had changed shape and texture and looked like a resin-rifle.

'Now I know where you get your name from,' said Emily in awe.

'Wow!' said Pete who couldn't stop staring. 'That's a brilliant power. I have to try that. Can you turn into famous people too?'

Chameleon arched an eyebrow. 'Yes. My power is online. I should know as I donated it.' Lorna nudged Toby in the ribs, Chameleon had proved her point about the origin of the powers. 'Now we can walk through the front door. I just need one of you to volunteer as a prisoner.'

Midges buzzed around the guards at the foot of the ramp. The weather was oppressively warm, even as the sun sank and they were in the shade afforded by the craft above them. They irritably swatted the flies and hoped they would be leaving soon for cooler climes.

Movement from across the field caught their attention. Another solider was escorting a young boy wearing glasses, and oddly, a wetsuit. The boy had his hands over his head and a resin-rifle pushed him along.

The ramp guard nodded towards the boy as they approached. 'What have you found?'

'This creep was sneaking around the perimeter. Thought Tempest might want a word with him.'

'He's just a kid.'

'Naw, he's a Super.'

At the mention of the word 'Super', both men gripped their rifles tighter and became instantly more alert.

'You sure?' asked the guard uncertainly. 'Doesn't look very super.'

'Certain. Unless every kid can fire lasers from his eyes.'

The guard licked his lips nervously. 'You're right. Boss best deal with him.'

The prisoner took several steps up the ramp.

''Ere, you can't go in there,' snapped the guard as he blocked his path.

But it was distraction enough for Chameleon to wheel around and lunged at the guards.

'Get the other one!' Chameleon bellowed.

Pete spun around and squinted; preparing to unleash the laser blast he *was certain* that he had downloaded.

The guard went ridged, expecting to be blasted apart. But Pete was the one who gasped as he was suddenly looking at a skeleton standing right in front of him.

At first he thought he'd killed the man - but when the skeleton brought his transparent rifle to bear, Pete knew what had happened. He'd insisted that they try their powers before leaving, but Lorna had been adamant that there was no time.

'What are you waiting for?' shouted Chameleon as he wrestled the other guard.

'I can't do anything... I've only got x-ray vision! I down-loaded the *wrong* power!'

FROM THEIR HIDING place in the trees, Toby, Lorna and Emily watched as Pete froze.

'Why is he hesitating?' said Emily with concern.

Toby knew the answer. 'He didn't download the power he wanted.'

Chameleon had fallen to the ground, struggling with the guard he held in a chokehold. Pete's opponent raised his gun ready to shoot point blank.

'No!' shrieked Emily. She burst from cover and instinctively extended her hand like she'd just thrown a ball. Two pulsing energy orbs shot from her palm, the spheres linked together by a cord of crackling electricity as they whirled through the air like bolas.

They snagged around the guard before he could pull the trigger, tightening around him like a coiling snake, pinning his arms to his side. His gun clattered to the floor as the breath was crushed from him, and he fell unconscious.

Chameleon picked himself up off the floor; his opponent

was frozen like a statue, a fine crystal-like coating covering him.

'You okay?' asked Chameleon with some concern.

'Yeah, I just got a useless superpower.'

'Nonsense, there's no such thing as a *useless* power,' said Chameleon haughtily. 'Every one has its uses, whether it's apparent or not'

The others joined them from across the field peering around to check patrolling guards hadn't spotted them. Chameleon transformed back into his pale self and gave Emily an appraising look.

'You did that? Most impressive.'

Emily beamed from the complement. Pete cleared his throat and pointed to the two prone guards.

'Shouldn't we hide them away so nobody notices?'

'Good thinking,' said Chameleon. 'Let's drag them inside. Hurry.'

It took two of them to haul the heavy guards up the ramp. The one Chameleon had struck was as stiff as a rod and easier to move, and Pete suspected he wasn't breathing either. Once they were stowed in a corridor on the ship, Chameleon waved them in. 'Follow me.'

Lorna and Emily followed without question. Pete and Toby brought up the rear. Pete whispered to his friend.

'Who put *him* in charge?'

The corridors were brightly lit and had a new, plastic sheen to them. They passed several closed doors and branching corridors, but Chameleon ignored them. Toby had the impression they were moving towards the centre of the disc shaped craft.

'You sure you know where we're heading?' he asked Chameleon as they paused at a junction.

'If you've seen one of these ships, you've seen them all. The assembly chamber is in the middle.'

'I haven't seen any security.'

'Oh, it's there,' said Chameleon looking cautiously around. It just doesn't know *we* are here. This way.'

They crossed a junction into a circular corridor that curved away either side. Toby assumed if he followed it he'd just loop back on himself. Chameleon paused at a door, then nodded.

'He's in there?'

'How can you tell?' asked Toby. He was getting irritated with this cocksure hero marshalling them around.

Pete stared at the door, and his gaze seemed to become unfocussed. 'He's right. I can see him now.'

'With that useless power, eh?' said Chameleon. 'Touch the door, and focus that x-ray vision.'

Pete did as he was asked. The door undulated like water and then suddenly became transparent, although every blemish on the door could still be seen like it was cast in glass. Everybody gasped, and Pete realized that they could all see through it too.

'Not bad eh?' said Chameleon as he peered beyond. 'Keep touching the door. And don't worry it's one-way. He can't see out.'

Doc Tempest sat in a circular room opposite eight massive screens. Each screen was suspended from the ceiling on segmented metal arms that allowed it to move around the room tilting them at any angle. This gave the chilling appearance that the shadowy faces on the screens were looking directly out at the world around them.

Doc Tempest was hunched in a high-back chair looking very worried as the faces surrounded him like predatory snakes. The sound seemed to carry through the x-rayed door as clearly as if the heroes were in the room.

'Your behaviour has been inappropriate Tempest,' snarled a dreary voice from one of the screens. 'So your information better be valuable.'

A woman's voice spoke up. 'We suspect Basilisk is planning to extract revenge on the Council. What have you to say?'

Lorna glances at Chameleon. 'Basilisk?'

'Long story. But he's somebody crazier than Tempest. The Council of Evil banished him for breaking their rules.'

'Rules?' asked Toby.

'Even bad guys need some rules to follow. But after the Council created Villain.net, things got—'

Pete looked up with interest. 'Whoa, there's a *villain* website too?'

'Of course, how do you think—?'

'Sssh,' snapped Lorna. 'Tempest's speaking.'

'I have given you enough information about Basilisk's plans. I risked my life to steal it from under his nose. He's working together with a boy.'

'We know of the boy. And your data has some merit. If it is true then Basilisk poses a risk to us all. He must be stopped.'

Chameleon gasped. 'Tempest's betraying his only ally! And we thought he was working directly *with* Basilisk. Ha! There certainly is no honour amongst thieves. This is a bad move for him. Great news for us.'

Toby nodded, although he didn't quite follow. It sounded like an espionage plot in a spy movie, using one villain to trap another. But what he did understand was that both Chameleon and the Council of Evil both wanted Basilisk and this *boy*. Toby wondered what kind of supervillain would cause such a manhunt.

Doc Tempest's gaze nervously flicked from screen-to-screen as they writhed around him. 'I have submitted my report, now please can I have my permit?'

'Very well, Tempest. The Council has decided your reconnaissance against Basilisk was sufficient. You have your permit for your scheme, and remember this time to pay your commission of whatever you extort to the Council.'

A look of relief flooded across Tempest's face. He shook his fist victoriously. 'Thank you. I'll make the wise Council proud of me I assure you!'

A flash of anger crossed Chameleon's face. 'I've heard enough. We'll stop this now. We'll arrest Tempest and find out where he is holding your mother.'

He pulled Pete away from the door. Immediately the material reverted to steel. Chameleon hit a control button on the wall and the door swished open. Chameleon stepped inside with the four heroes behind in their best fighting stance.

'End of the line, Tempest!'

Doc Tempest's face dropped in shock. All eight monitors swivelled to face the intruders. Although none of the faces were discernible, the variety of oddly shaded silhouetted heads sent a shiver of fear down Lorna's spine. Tempest then saw Toby and Lorna and he glowered.

'You! Come a step closer and I swear I'll kill your mother!'

'Intruders!' shouted one of the screen entities in a gurgling voice. Immediately a siren whooped throughout the ship.

Doc Tempest pushed both hands forward and a wall of

shimmering ice shot towards the group. In the blink of an eye, Chameleon leapt towards the wall - his whole body transformed into a slender, yellow-scaled lizard, his face a bizarre hybrid of lizard and man. With his sharp reptilian claws he skittered effortlessly up the wall.

The children didn't have time to run. Lorna pushed forward and silently hoped she had selected the right power. A giant bubble blossomed around them, protecting them as the ice smashed harmlessly against it. It took all of Lorna's concentration to keep the shield in place for those few seconds. Her legs trembled and the moment she hesitated the bubble popped - shattering the ice that had formed across it.

Tempest's gaze followed Chameleon across the wall, the monitors swivelling to watch his progress too. Tempest fired a volley of electrical bolts from his fingers and tore the ceiling behind Chameleon - accidentally blasting two of the monitor arms, sending then crashing to the floor in a shower of sparks. Chameleon, who was holding on to one of the arms, fell with it.

An automated voice echoed across the ship. 'Intruder alert! Beginning auto-destruct. Waiting for confirmation.'

'No!' screamed Tempest. 'Not *destruct* you idiots!'

Council of Evil technicians were notoriously bad at maintaining equipment and labelling the correct buttons. Back at his base, the lax Council staff that he had hired always got auto-launch and auto-destruct the wrong way around. They had even marked the manual-override buttons incorrectly.

The entire structure rumbled, throwing Lorna to the floor. Toby gripped the doorjamb for support. Doc Tempest had Chameleon pinned by the throat, a look of murder contorting his face.

'This will teach you to spy on me!'

Tempest's fingers turned white as frost clung to them. The frost spread out across Chameleon's throat, and up towards his head. Chameleon's reptilian form sprung back to his regular human shape, but Tempest didn't relinquish his grip as the frost spread. Chameleon lashed out in panic and smashed Tempest's wristband from his arm. The electronic gadget skittered across the room as the ship lurched to one side. Tempest noticed the touch display read: CONFIRM AUTO-DESTRUCT: YES/NO - just as it bounced, hitting the 'yes' option.

'Auto-destruct sequence activated!' said the measured electronic voice.

Toby and Pete lunged forward - their combined weight shoved Tempest off Chameleon. The three of them slid into the wall as the floor tipped beneath them.

'We're taking off', Emily shouted.

Toby nimbly sprang on top of Tempest and gripped his collar.

'Where's my mother?'

Tempest flashed his fanged teeth and grabbed Toby's hands - the touch was intensely cold and needles of pain shot up Toby's arm before they went numb. Tempest threw him off, and effortlessly shoved Pete away as he climbed to his feet.

'You will all die here!' snarled Tempest, 'Blown to smithereens!' He rapidly clapped his hands like a spoilt child. 'Isn't that great!' he whooped before spinning towards the doorway.

Emily barred his path her hands already glowing from the forming energy bolas. The whole ship violently shook like they'd hit severe turbulence, and Emily lost her balance as the bolas spun out - Tempest bent backwards as it passed centimetres over his head and slammed into the wall.

'Not today, little girl,' he sneered and raced from the room.

Toby rubbed warmth into his hands but still couldn't feel anything. Chameleon sprang to his feet, rubbing the warmth back to his throat. He hoisted Pete up.

'We have to leave,' Chameleon said in a hoarse voice.

Emily and Toby pulled Lorna to her feet. They ran into the corridor as the sound of tearing metal reverberated through the ship. Cracks ran across the floor and ceiling and the group stopped in their tracks as the corridor ahead suddenly disappeared as a massive chunk of the ship ripped away right in front of them, revealing nothing but twilight sky.

The craft was self-destructing in the air - the ground spinning far below. The sky was full of flaming debris as the ship fell apart. Flying through the falling wreckage would be like navigating through a minefield.

'We're trapped!' wailed Pete.

'Grab on to me!' screamed Chameleon as another section of the floor ahead gave way. 'All of you, think of Toby's house. Imagine it in your minds *now!*'

Everybody latched onto Chameleon as the roof was torn away in a fiery explosion. Toby scrunched his eyes and heard an explosive thunderclap, and a wave of dizziness struck him.

When he looked around he saw that they were all laying in his garden, the familiar oak tree was behind them.

'What happened?' asked Lorna as she got her bearings.

'Teleportation,' Emily answered knowingly.

Chameleon stood up, dusting himself off. 'The Council initiated a self-destruct sequence. We had to get out of there.

Is this where you live?' he asked with a note of doubt as he studied the remains of the house covered in plastic sheeting.

'Yeah,' Toby answered. 'That's my home. What's left of it.'

Chameleon gave Pete and Toby a look of gratitude. 'You saved my life back there. If it weren't for you, Tempest would have killed me for sure. You really do have the courage that makes a hero. All of you.'

'Any time,' said Pete, trying to stand as heroically as possible despite feeling nauseous.

Chameleon stared at the remains of Pete's improvised superhero costume. 'But I think you should reconsider your outfit.'

Toby sighed deeply, making Chameleon hesitate.

'So we're on our own again?'

'You have the Hero community at your fingertips. You're not alone.'

'Feels like. We seem to keep failing.'

Chameleon looked at each of them. 'You have come from being ordinary people, with ordinary lives and you are slowly becoming true heroes. It's a path with many obstacles ahead, and many challenges to face. But you must remember that being a hero is not about winning or losing. It's about courage and doing the right thing against the temptation to take the path of least resistance. When you have faced that final challenge, then you will have risen to the status of hero.'

Toby mulled over the words.

Chameleon continued. 'I'm sorry we couldn't apprehend Tempest today. But I assure you, the moment I discover anything about the location of your mother, I will let you know.'

Chameleon teleported away with a bang.

Toby looked at his friends dejectedly. 'What a complete waste of time that was.'

'Oh, it hasn't been a *complete* waste,' said Pete. 'I think we'll be able to track Tempest, without mister know-it-all, if we get this thing working.'

He held up Doc Tempest's broken wristband.

Sarah Wilkinson sat in a rail-pod that shot through a tunnel system. She was starting to feel weak. After pleading with a solider, she got word to Tempest that she needed her insulin shots, but he was unsympathetic to her condition.

A bored looking guard sat opposite Sarah. He seemed more intent on pulling at his tight uniform that was riding up his bum than anything else. At one point the dark walls of the tunnel gave way to glass and she saw an awe-inspiring view; an immense snowfield stretching as far as the eye could see. Then they were plunged back into darkness.

She had been kept in the hangar for almost two hours while the guards patched up the damage caused by the superheroes. She was glad for the change of surrounding, but it was no more than a minute before they arrived at their destination. The guard shoved her up a corridor carved from solid ice, metal grids on the floor prevented Sarah from slipping. She shivered against the cold, but noticed small heating ducts were blowing in warm air. She was led to a small cell; furnished with nothing but a bed and a single fluorescent tube for light. He uncuffed her hands and shoved her inside.

Sarah sat on the edge of the bed, no longer feeling scared, but angry instead. She thought of her husband out somewhere in Mexico, and then Lorna and Toby. She hoped somebody was looking after them. They couldn't look after themselves.

Toby was tired but unable to sleep. He was worried about his mother - not just how they'd get her back, but mainly about her insulin. Without it she could die.

Tempest's threats constantly replayed every time he closed his eyes. Through heavy eyelids, he examined Doc Tempest's digital wristband. He wondered how they could use it to find his mother, but no matter how much he poked and prodded he couldn't get the thing working. He put it down and lay flat on the uncomfortable air mattress; what he wouldn't give to be back in his own bed... with his mother safely home.

Staring at the array of posters on Pete's wall, strategically positioned to hide the peeling wallpaper, Toby felt a wave of regret about every argument he'd ever had with his mother. At the time the fights seemed justified and important - but in the grand scheme of things he could now see every argument was just a waste of time. And if they didn't rescue her in time and Tempest killed her... then he would never have the chance to say sorry.

He refused to cry. Instead he listened to the elephant like snores coming from Pete and, for the first time, he envied his friend. Pete's parents may always be struggling for money, but at least they were safe and sound and not in the hands of a megalomaniac...

Lorna couldn't sleep either. She had her own room at Emily's which was comfortable, but it wasn't home. Lorna realized that she was feeling homesick. She climbed out of bed and crept downstairs into the kitchen to get a glass of milk. She was surprised to find Emily already at the kitchen table staring thoughtfully at her own drink.

'Can't sleep,' said Lorna. She didn't have the strength for a more detailed explanation.

'Me either. I just kept going over today's events in my mind. It didn't seem so scary at the time... but now, I feel terrified being up there as the ship broke apart.'

Lorna poured her drink and sat opposite her friend, both keeping their voices low so they didn't wake anyone.

'I suppose it hasn't sunk for me,' said Lorna. 'Not yet anyway. I just keep feeling... responsible for everything that's happening to mum.'

Emily shook her head. Her parents had raised her to see the world logically. She knew that with hindsight anybody could blame themselves for almost anything. Why hadn't they been at home to stop Tempest? Why did they download the superpowers in the first place? The list was endless, but Emily knew they could only act now to affect the future.

'You're not responsible, Lorn. Doc Tempest is. And we are going to save your mum. No matter how difficult it's going to be.'

Lorna managed a smile. Even though Emily was wearing ridiculous pink pyjamas, she still made sense. Tomorrow would undoubtedly bring a new, unexpected, adventure. And, hopefully, a step closer to ending this nightmare.

Toby was forced to school by Pete's parents who insisted that it would be 'good for him'. Toby sensed that he was getting under their feet. He suspected too that they normally spent their time arguing and not being able to do so in front of him was adding to the strain.

At lunchtime Toby and Pete sat in the corner of the canteen picking at their food as they examined Tempest's wristband. No matter how he pressed and poked nothing seemed to activate it. Only when Pete placed it on his wrist to see if it would suit him, did the gizmo suddenly lit up like a Christmas tree.

'What did you do?' asked Toby.

'Just put it on. Maybe that powers it?'

The broken screen flashed the message STORM ENGINE: FULL THROTTLE.

'Storm Engine?' echoed Pete. 'Isn't that what Tempest called his *wever* control machine?' He smirked at the villain's mispronunciation.

'At least we know this thing is still connected to his network. It's a pity we can't find a way to make it stop the Storm Engine. But I reckon if we can somehow trace the signal, we can find my mum.'

Pete was keeping a watchful glance for Jake Hunter and his gang, who were all mercifully absent. He noticed Lorna and Emily approaching. They looked more cheerful than they should be. They sat in the plastic seats opposite and whispered conspiratorially.

'We've found Tempest!' stated Lorna.

Toby held the fork half way to his mouth, the food now forgotten. 'Where? How did you do that?'

'He's heading towards Florida,' said Lorna in a harsh whisper. 'Em and used the computers in school to check out the Internet news. That's when we saw the hurricane!'

'It formed unnaturally quickly and moving faster than

anything else on record,' Emily added in breathless excitement. 'Almost like it has been artificially created!'

Pete's eyes went wide and he showed them the activated wristband. 'The Storm Engine! That's how he created the tornado and hurricane!'

'Which he then uses as cover for his attacks,' Toby added thoughtfully. 'What's in Florida?'

'Theme parks? Some great roller coasters,' said Pete.

'Not the kind of thing you'd expect Tempest to steal though,' said Toby.

'Does it matter?' snapped Lorna. 'Point is, we know where he'll be! Find him, we can find mum!'

Toby nodded, feeling the sudden fire of adventure in his stomach. It was Pete's voice that brought him back down to earth.

'One problem - we're in school. We can't possibly leave now.'

'Why not?' asked Toby.

'It's not right! I felt bad enough skipping school yesterday. If we get caught—'

'We need to find Tempest in order to find our mother!' Toby shot back, a little louder than he intended, attracting attention from around the canteen. He lowered his voice. 'The police wouldn't believe us, and right now the only thing that has been of use is the Hero website. We have to skip the afternoon. After all this is over, we can explain and people will understand.'

Pete looked doubtful. 'If my parents found out, they wouldn't be so understanding. Trust me on that. Maybe I should stay here?' Pete didn't dare look up. Instead, he closely examined the wristband, avoiding anybody's gaze. He was feeling torn between not risking antagonising his parents, who seemed to be less a part of his life than his friends, and the selfish fact that he was afraid of getting hurt. Years of being at the end of Jake Hunter's fist had made him a coward.

Toby looked at his friend in shock. This was the second time Pete need persuading. He was beginning to doubt the strength of their friendship. 'You're not going to help? We need you! We're a team!'

Emily grabbed Pete's arm. 'Pete, please. This is for your friends! We need you.'

Pete looked at Toby, whose face was grave, and then to Lorna who nodded encouragingly. Drawing a deep breath he nodded, making his decision against his own better judgement.

'Okay. Let's do it.'

Toby exhaled a long breath and patted Pete on the back, but he couldn't summon the words to thank him.

The four of them got up and cleared the table before discreetly heading towards the school gates. Freedom was just a few more steps.

'Toby Wilkinson!' a deep voice shouted.

Toby froze mid-stride. The Headmaster, Mr Harris, must have been in his late fifties, and was shaped roughly like an egg. When his voice boomed across the school, it was usually because *somebody* was in trouble. Mr Harris walked over to them, wheezing heavily, his hand raised in the air as though he was about to hail a taxi.

'Sir?' said Toby as casually as he possibly could, and wondered if he had some kind of truant radar.

The headmaster scrutinized the motley crew as he caught his breath. Like a magician's trick, a handkerchief appeared in his hand and he dabbed the sweat from his brow.

'Ah... the Wilkinsons. I see you're heading, um, home. I mean... um... wherever it is that you're both staying.'

'Er...' was all Toby could manage. What could he possibly say? That they were on their way home to download superpowers, in order to stop a supervillain from destroying Florida with his Storm Engine, so they could rescue their kidnapped mother? Somehow, Toby thought, Mr Harris wouldn't believe him.

'Good,' said Mr Harris.

It took a moment for Toby to process what he'd just heard. 'Good?'

Mr Harris didn't hear as he dabbed his brow again. 'Your father has both Emily's and Pete's numbers, and was very eager to speak to you both.'

Lorna stepped forward. 'You've heard from dad?'

'Yes, of course,' said Mr Harris, a sudden crease of suspicion forming on his sweaty brow. 'I thought you knew, that's why you're—'

Toby seized the moment. 'Of course, Lorn. I just didn't want to tell you, in case you got overexcited. He's called, isn't that right sir?'

Mr Harris nodded. 'Yes, yes. Well, off you go. Don't keep him waiting!'

It was now obvious to Toby his father was not a superhero otherwise he would have flown to their aide. And he saw little point in talking to him now that they seemed close to tracking their mother down. When they arrived at Pete's house both Toby and Pete had decided to avoid answering the phone. Instead they booted up the computer and headed straight for the Hero site.

'Wait,' said Emily. 'Go to the news first.'

'Why?'

'I just want to know how bad that storm is.'

Pete navigated to the BBC world news site. The main story was the unnaturally fast-forming storm that was raging across America, which had in fact completely skipped Florida without causing any damage. Weather forecaster were baffled as they showed a satellite image tracking the storm over Alabama - and it was *still* not causing damage as the sinister black clouds zoomed northwards.

'So he's not going for Florida,' said Lorna, twirling her hair thoughtfully.

'What's in Alabama?' asked Pete.

'Banks? A big bank?' said Toby.

'The biggest...' mumbled Emily under her breath. 'Budge over.'

Emily slid half onto Pete's seat until he gave it up and stood next to her.

'What're you doing?' he asked, a little peeved that he had been pushed off his own computer.

'Looking for something,' said Emily thoughtfully. She suddenly tapped the screen. 'Here!'

'Don't touch the screen, you'll dirty it,' complained Pete even though the screen was filled with his own greasy fingerprints.

Lorna read out. 'Fort Knox?'

'Yeah,' said Emily. 'It holds gold for the U.S. Government - and it's in Kentucky!'

'Not Alabama?' asked Toby.

'No, but look!' Emily called up a map of the storm and pointed. They all saw it immediately. 'The storm's heading in a straight line - right for Fort Knox!'

'He's going to perform the biggest theft *ever*!' said Toby.

'And we're going to stop him,' declared Emily. She stood and patted Pete on the shoulder. 'Pete, it's your turn. Get us to the Hero website.'

Pleased to be doing something again, Pete took the seat and called up the mysterious website. They were greeted by a flashing message:

MISSION IN PROGRESS: YOU HAVE FAILED TASK ONE.

Everybody swapped worried glances.

'What does that mean?' asked Pete.

Toby understood. 'It means we wasted our free powers on Tempest in France. Click on the powers, let's see what happens.'

Pete selected the icon to enter the page of downloadable powers. The computer made a warning noise and flashed another message:

YOU HAVE NO HEROIC POINTS. DO YOU WISH TO PURCHASE POWERS? YES/NO.

'How are we going to pay for that?' wailed Lorna. 'We have no money!'

Pete looked at his friends, every one of them wearing a look of panic.

'Chameleon mentioned an instruction page,' Emily reminded them.

'We haven't got time for that now,' Toby snapped. 'They want paying!'

'Come on, there's got to be a way out of this,' said Pete.

'Like what?' Emily asked. She pulled a handful of coins from her pocket. There was just enough to buy a magazine perhaps, certainly not superpowers. 'We can't do it! Doc

Tempest is going to steal billions of dollars in gold - and we can't *afford* to stop him! That's ironic!'

Pete snorted. His was just typical of his luck. 'So we just give up? Em, can't you just ask your parents for money? They're loaded aren't they?'

'Of course not!'

Lorna kicked at the floor in anger. 'What else can we do?'

'Guys,' said Toby. A thought had just occurred to him. 'We're richer than you think.'

'What do you mean?' asked Lorna suspiciously.

'Pete, we need to take the computer outside. I know somebody who can help us!'

FORT KNOX_

Mr Patel's grocery store never seemed to close. It was open when Toby and Lorna started their delivery round even on a lazy weekend morning, and lights burned from inside whenever they passed it at night. Today was no exception. Mr Patel turned to greet his new customers with a polite 'Good afternoon'. But his face split into a grin when he recognised Toby and Lorna.

'Ah, my friends, what brings you here today?' His pursed his lips when he glanced at his watch. 'And shouldn't you be in school?' He looked curiously at Pete who was surreptitiously carrying his computer casing under a thick black bin bag, which he rested on the floor with a tired sigh.

'We've had time off, Mr Patel,' said Toby with his most sorrowful expression. 'Our house got trashed by a tornado and our mother's... missing.'

Mr Patel's face softened, and he wrung his hands anxiously. 'Of course, I heard about that. I'm so sorry. Please take a chocolate bar or snack in my condolences.' True to form, Mr Patel began handing out sweets.

'No thank you,' said Lorna. The others following her lead in refusing the offer, except Pete, who snagged a bag of crisps. Emily shot him a disgusted look. Pete shrugged.

'What? I'm hungry.'

Lorna continued. 'Actually we wanted to talk about our pay?'

'Ah,' said Mr Patel, slapping his forehead as if to reboot his memory. 'Certainly. I think we're a little backed up, are we not?' He headed around to his till to open the cash draw. 'And it would be bad business to lose my best delivery team.'

'It's not cash we want,' said Toby just as the cash draw shot out to a jingle of loose coins.

Mr Patel brightened. 'Oh? Not sweets and not cash. This is a happy day. Then what?'

'Actually we wanted you to purchase something for us from the Internet.'

Mr Patel's eyes narrowed in suspicion once more. 'The *Internet*?'

Toby nodded. Lorna lightly tapped the computer with her toe.

'And you have to promise to keep it a secret,' she added.

'Hero?' said Mr Patel staring at the screen. 'Is this some kind of game? Or a comic perhaps?'

'Well it's a lot of fun,' said Pete. He looked at Toby and faltered. 'Well, it can be.'

They all looked expectantly at the website. Pete had hooked up his computer to the old monitor Mr Patel used to track his shop's accounts. Toby and Lorna exchanged nervous glances; they had planned to keep the website a secret, but it was unavoidable for them to have to show it to

Mr Patel. They just hoped he wouldn't ask too many questions so they could keep the superpowers quiet.

But, like most adults, Mr Patel simply didn't see the 'big picture'. He already had his spectacles balanced on the edge of his nose, and was staring at his credit card.

'Okay, this is your money,' said Mr Patel. 'You can spend it how you wish, I suppose.' The tone of his voice indicated he disapproved of such frivolous wastes such as computer games.

Pete clicked through the screen, and got the online donations page up. 'There you go. Just type your credit card details in there, and the amount here. Put the whole lot in.'

'Hold on,' said Emily holding her hand to stop Mr Patel. 'Let's just check the website is secure. Look here, this padlock symbol on the browser means there's a security certificate...' She trailed off as Mr Patel's confused expression. 'Well, it just means it's safe, so we're good to go. Let's just hope the website doesn't just steal the money.'

'Don't be daft,' said Pete. 'These are the *good* guys. Hate to buy anything from that villain site. I imagine you'd get ripped off there!'

Mr Patel began slowly copying his details onto the computer.

'Thanks for doing this,' said Lorna.

The shopkeeper peered over the top of his glasses in a way that reminded Emily of her grandfather. 'And you're sure? The whole amount to be transferred?' he asked.

'Yes. Everything.'

Mr Patel counted off on his fingers, mumbling under his breath. 'Two months, eight weekends... that's...' He typed the amount into the computer; looked at Pete and Lorna for confirmation. Then he hit the ENTER button. The website beeped and the page suddenly changed to read: WELCOME BACK HEROES.

Toby gripped Mr Patel's hand and shook it eagerly. 'You don't know how much this means to us! Thank you!' He nudged Pete with his foot. 'Hurry up, unhook your computer - we've got to get back to yours to... er... *play*.'

'Going as fast as I can,' grumbled Pete as he carefully shut down the computer.

Mr Patel watched the four teenagers scurry out of the shop as quickly as they could. He shook his head; it was such a shame kids of today spent all their time sitting in front of a computer screen, and never really getting to see the big wide world outside.

With their new finances secured, the gang browsed through the range of powers on offer as soon as they returned to Pete's.

'Is it me, or are there *more* choices than usual?'

Emily had been thinking the same thing. She stopped Pete before he rashly chose something.

'Don't click *anything*,' she warned.

Toby was impatient. Both he and Lorna had been watching the news - and the hurricane was already bearing down on its target. 'There's no way we can make it there in time. Even flying!'

'Hold on,' said Emily, still studying the screen. 'I just want to see if there's a pattern to all these icons.'

'Em,' said Lorna, 'We're running out of time!'

'Well you won't let me read the instructions and we have to make sure we don't download useless powers. Plus, we're paying for them so we can download *more* than one each!'

'No way!' cried Pete. 'How do you know that?'

'Says so right here.' Emily tapped the screen. 'If you bother reading it.'

'Cool!'

Lorna shook her head. 'We're going to have to move like lightning to get there.'

Emily nodded. 'Then the bad news is that we'll have to teleport.'

If anybody was walking casually by, they would have heard a thunderclap immediately followed by four confused looking children appearing from thin air, one of whom staggered dizzily before falling to his knees and taking off his glasses in case he threw up.

Fortunately there was nobody around to see the heroes' unorthodox arrival. They stood awed by the swirling mass of clouds that congealed into the visible wall of a hurricane in the distance. It was enormous, dwarfing the tornado storm that ravaged their home. The clouds stretched towards the ground and swept towards them at an incredible speed, and with a constant rumble generated by the high winds. Even from so far away it pushed at them with such fury that they had to angle their bodies against the wind and shout to be heard.

Toby helped Pete stand. 'You okay?'

Pete wiped his mouth with his sleeve. This time he had agreed with Toby and ditched the superhero costume for a jumper and jeans. 'I hate the feeling teleportation gives!' He had felt giddy, like spinning on the spot for thirty minutes but all condensed into a second.

Toby glanced at his watch. 'Well, it got us here in five seconds!'

'Where's *here*?'

Lorna nudged them both. She was staring behind them. They all turned to see—

'Fort Knox,' said Lorna with relief, and remembering it from a picture on the net. 'Right on target!'

Spread around them was a sprawling military base, set on gentle undulating hills. Fort Knox itself was a simple, white-washed square building made of two levels, very much like a concrete birthday cake. It was unimpressive considering the wealth it held inside.

Twelve olive-green M1 Abrams tanks had circled the compound beyond a chain-linked fence that had already been blown flat by the Herculean winds. The tanks' turrets pointed into the maelstrom.

The gale was growing stronger by the second, and almost pushed the heroes off their feet. They held their ground and saw movement in the clouds. Dark elongated shapes were just visible - two massive floating structures.

'Here he comes,' yelled Lorna.

'Let's get straight in there and get Tempest,' shouted Toby firmly. 'If he doesn't talk about where he's holding mum, then we'll knock it out of him!'

He leapt forward, and soared into the air. The others followed close behind - the wind almost blew them away like feathers, but they stabilised themselves and pushed into the storm.

They had learnt from their past mistakes in fighting Tempest, and this time they were prepared for *anything*.

Or so they hoped.

. . .

Struggling towards the hurricane, they could see beyond the cloud wall a mile-wide tract of land that lead into the distance - the path of devastation wrought by Doc Tempest's weather control. It was a massive amount of damage just so that he could rob a bank.

In seconds the team had punctured through the leading edge of the hurricane. The cyclonic winds threatened to pull them sidelong - but they persevered into the calm of the storm's eye and into sudden perfect weather.

Doc Tempest's army greeted them. Two huge floating barges, approximately the length of battleships, floated on a cushion of air. Their wide, flat decks had obviously been designed to stack enormous quantities of gold bars. But what the heroes didn't expect were the massive domes - about the size of a house - mounted on the front of the crafts. A huge barrel poked from the housing - it was unmistakably a gun turret, which spun with a whirl of hydraulics to face them.

But that was the least of their problems.

Some forty glyder-discs zigzagged through the air like flies. Hulking mercenaries, in their skin-tight uniforms, were riding on each arm with resin-rifles. They instantly detected the new arrivals and bore down on the four kids like a swarm of killer bees.

Doc Tempest was on his own skiff, circling above the flying armada. His voice boomed from speakers mounted on every craft.

'You again? Don't you get the message? Was my hint too subtle? You fools think you can challenge me? Well listen closely - for bothering me one time too many, I will execute my hostage! Do I make myself clear? Whoa, but I just remembered' Tempest slapped his enormous forehead with the palm of his hand. 'That won't matter because you'll be *dead*!

Lorna hovered. The others hung around her, bobbing like humming birds as Tempest's forces closed in on them.

'He's going to kill mum if we do anything!' she cried.

Toby grabbed his sister's arm. 'He could do that *anytime*. And it's good news he hasn't already. Must mean he thinks we're a real threat! We have to stop him!'

Lorna shot her brother a furious look. 'How can you be so reckless with her life? Just because you both argue all the time doesn't mean you can do that!'

'What? Arguing has nothing to do with anything! Just that *you're* her favourite—'

BOOM! A shockwave struck the undercarriage of one of the giant carriers, ripping a car-sized hole in it. Black smoke poured from the lesion, but the impact did little to halt the carrier. More rib-shaking booms followed in rapid succession, and Toby only became aware of Pete shouting as one of the goon's glyder-disc exploded into a million pieces.

'The tanks in Fort Knox! They're firing!' screamed Pete.

Toby and Lorna exchanged glances - they were right in the line of fire!

In retaliation, the massive dome-turrets on Doc Tempest's barges swept downwards and fired a volley of blinding slivers of energy.

Below, a couple of M1 tanks were hit full on; the armoured behemoths spun through the air as their gun-turrets were ripped away. The remaining tanks started to move in a grinding of gears, two colliding head on, armour buckling. But they hadn't scattered far enough—

The hurricane was on them as the second volley of shots came from Tempest's barges. The remaining tanks were batted away - two bursting into flames, the crews escaping only to be swept off their feet by the strength of the winds and thrown a dozen meters as the hurricane chewed the electrified fences.

The artificially induced force of nature had reached Fort Knox.

Alarms shrieked across the complex - but there was nobody left to respond to them. Brickwork began to crumble; cracks started to race across the bulletproof windows as the air pressure increased.

A sudden mass of thick, sticky blobs sprung from the approaching soldier's rifles, whizzing past the heroes' heads with high-pitched whines.

Lorna and Toby shot straight up to avoid the attack; Emily and Pete peeled off either side as about twenty glyder-discs streamed past them. Toby glanced around - the remaining troopers had descended towards the roof of Fort Knox, which was being torn off by the relentless winds. The troopers themselves seemed unaffected by the winds, protected by a nullifying field around the glyder-discs, which appeared as a faint energy crackle. Within seconds the roof had given way completely - and Tempest's men disappeared inside.

Toby dragged his eyes back to the skies as a pair of glyders banked towards him, the henchmen readying their weapons. Toby extended his hands as a hot rush raked through each arm, down to his fingertips—

WHOOSH! Fireballs the size of basketballs shot from his hands; they hit one of the glyder-discs and hacked it in two. The surprised thug trod air for a second before plummeting, the gun in his hand firing wildly. A stray shot struck one of the glyder-discs forcing it away from colliding with

Emily. The glue bullet expanded on the underside of the glyder, throwing its balance - the man on board was flung away as the glyder-disc flipped like a coin and plummeted earthward.

The second platform made an emergency climb, away from the boy with flaming hands.

Emily had no idea what powers she had downloaded. She couldn't even decide if the icon she clicked on was a stickman running or leaping. Either way she had about three seconds to discover what it was. She tensed her body and zoomed towards the three glyder-discs bearing down on her. She could feel a soothing warm glow radiate from the pit of her stomach, as if she had drunk warm soup on a winter's day.

As Pete watched, Emily's clothes, skin, and waving strands of blond hair seemed to shimmer like polished silver. She seemed to become denser.

Emily extended her hands, trusting *something* unusual would happen. As she did so, she noticed her hands and arms were shiny chrome - but she had no time to marvel at the fact before she crashed into the lead glyder.

Emily shot through it - she didn't feel the impact, but the platform exploded around her - and she continued in a straight line, blasting through two more platforms behind.

She had become a human bullet!

'She's so cool!' said Pete. He dragged his eyes away from Emily. A glyder-disc was zeroing in on him in a barrage of resin-bullets. He easily zigzagged the streams and squinted hard at his attacker. Instead of the laser blast he was expecting, he farted loudly. The noise startled the grim-faced thug so much that he pulled up short and burst into laughter - giving Pete the chance to get it right second time.

'Please… no more x-ray vision!' he murmured.

Intense rays of light blasted from his eyes, striking the platform and another behind it as he moved his gaze.

'Wow! Look what I can do!' he screamed triumphantly.

He turned to search for Toby - and the beams continued to blast from his eyes, inadvertently cutting down two of the thugs manoeuvring behind his friend. Toby spun around - and ducked - just as Pete's laser vision sliced narrowly over his head, gouging lines in the enormous barge behind him.

'Pete! Watch what you're doing!'

'Sorry!' said Pete, forcing himself to blink and stop the beams. When he opened his eyes the world was blurry. Had the superpower suddenly made him blind?

Panic stricken, he removed his glasses to clean them. His fingers went through the frames. Holding them up he could see the lasers had burnt perfect holes through the glass lenses.

'Oh, damn!' he cried.

Everything was a blur. Toby, Emily and Lorna were indistinguishable from the other figures flying around. A disc-glyder banked towards him at a furious speed. Pete reacted on instinct and shot his laser blast at the approaching enemy - only registering a figure between him and his target at the very last second.

'Lorna!' he screamed, but she didn't hear him.

In a confusing bur of activity the disc exploded as his laser blast struck. A furious cloud of orange flames chewed up the glyder - the solider riding it fell dozens of feet, miraculously landing on top of another disc swooping below. Pete's heart was pounded as he scanned the skies, but he couldn't see Lorna.

He must have killed her.

Pete was horrified, but before he could think what else to do, a powerful blow struck him in the back, and he was flung head-over-heels. His head hit something solid.

Pete staggered to his feet and was surprised to see a wall of gold. It took him seconds to get his bearings and realize he was standing on one of the barge decks. The other hung in the sky above him. The gold was being loaded fast by the mercenaries on their glyders. It already covered an area about a third the size of a football pitch. It was stacked in high blocks, with narrow aisles between them.

'Thought you could fight me again, worm?' said a familiar voice that made Pete spin around.

Doc Tempest was several meters away. It was obviously him who had slammed Pete onto the barge. Any reply from Pete was swallowed as he noticed a vortex of whirling air and gold bricks dropping above his head.

Pete dived aside as the mass descended slowly to the deck, landing where he had been standing seconds before. Gold whirled inside the vortex, which was generated by a goon's glyder floating above. It had sucked up gold bricks in a miniature whirlwind, literally vacuumed up the gold to be deposited in relatively neat blocks on the barge. Worry about Lorna temporarily disappeared as Pete marvelled at the villain's ingenuity.

His eyes lingered on the gold, which gleamed almost hypnotically - just one bar was worth more than his family owned... had *ever* owned.

'Ah, I see a familiar gleam in your eyes, boy. A poor boy shown the wealth of a nation,' gloated Tempest. 'Think if you had one, no, *ten* of those bars. Think how rich you would be.'

Pete stared at Tempest. Even without his glasses, he could see the veins under the villain's skin pulsing.

'The rich don't get bullied. They don't have sleepless nights worrying about paying the next bill. They can have *anything* they want, *do* anything they want. It's yours. Take it. A gift from me. All you have to do is help me and get rid of your toy-hero pals.'

The thought of living in riches floated through Pete's brain; a life of luxury would be worth a *few* sacrifices. He traced his hand across the gold.

'That's a very tempting offer,' said Pete as he traced his hand across the gold. It felt cool and soft. With money like this, he could ditch school and the bullies; live in his own place without his parents' misery to deal with.

No more arguments. No more crying himself to sleep.

'It's the real deal,' purred Tempest. 'You could afford laser surgery to your eyes. No more squinting or horrible nicknames.'

Pete remembered a proverb: money doesn't buy happiness. Somebody who really didn't know what wealth could buy must have come up with that phrase. Pete was pretty sure he'd be a lot happier. And if not happier, it would certainly buy him a better standard of misery. He thought of Lorna. Nothing would alleviate the fear he was feeling about her. Is she *was* dead Toby would never forgive him. He might as well be guilty and rich, rather than guilty and poor.

Tempest was beginning to get impatient as the remains of a burning glyder clattered down on the barge just metres away.

'Hurry up, I haven't got all day,' he said. 'What d'you think I am, a bank? Make up your mind.'

Pete met Tempest's gaze; his life changing decision had been made.

'That is a generous offer... but does that mean I would

have to look as ugly as you? I mean, what happened to your head to make it look like that?'

Even out of focus, Pete could see Tempest's face twist into a snarl of anger.

'Fool!' screamed Doc Tempest and levelled his arm at Pete.

Pete jumped to his feet and ran, as lightning spewed from Doc Tempest's fingers and raked across the barge's deck, leaving black scorch marks. Pete could feel the heat of the electricity on the back of his legs. He ducked into the golden aisles, hoping he could lose the villain.

In the sky above the carrier craft, Emily looked around, suddenly aware she hadn't seen Lorna for a while. She slid sideways to avoid a mass of glue-bullets and spurred forward towards the henchman that had fired at her. In retaliation she crunched through his platform like a knife through butter. The bewildered man gripped half a glyder-disc as it pirouetted earthward.

She glanced back at the barge in time to see Pete running from Doc Tempest's lightning attack. Her first instinct was to swoop down and help him - but then she noticed the second carrier was wheeling its gun turrets around to point them in Toby's direction.

Clenching her chrome fingers she took a second to bask in the warmth of the superpowers that flowed through her. In that moment of calm, Emily hatched a plan.

Toby was having a little too much fun as he flew in wide arcs, easily out-running the resin-blobs that whizzed past him. Too fast and agile for the glyders to keep up, he chose to remain a moving target, shooting fireballs so rapidly that it looked as though the sky was raining flame.

Toby saw Doc Tempest chasing Pete across the deck of

the gold-laden barge. Pete was lost from of view between the stacks of bullion.

'Pete!' With a roar, Toby accelerated towards the barge.

Pete held his breath, fearing the slightest wheeze would alert Doc Tempest to his presence.

'Come out, come out wherever you are, boy,' taunted Tempest.

Pete reached a crossroads of narrow passages between the gold. Tempest could be standing just around the corner.

'Only rats and cockroaches hide. Heroes fight!' Tempest's voice drifted down the aisle.

'But you're no hero, are you?'

This time the voice was an icy whisper, close to his ear. Pete spun around in fear, but no one was there... then, with a sinking feeling, he peered *up*.

Doc Tempest was hovering above him with a faint roar from his rocket boots, a sour grin on his face and his fingers out-stretched, ready to strike. 'Say goodbye to the riches you could have had!' sneered Tempest. 'In fact, say goodbye to *life*!'

Pete pressed himself against a bullion wall, waiting for the blast - when a ball of flame suddenly threw Doc Tempest sideways.

Toby swooped over the blocks of gold, cheering as his fireball dropped Doc Tempest onto the deck.

Toby hovered over Pete. 'You okay?'

Pete leapt into the air and floated alongside. He nodded, but avoiding meeting Toby's gaze.

'Yeah... but I broke my glasses, and I can't see very well.'

'What kind of superhero breaks his glasses?' exclaimed

Toby.

'The rubbish kind!' snarled Doc Tempest as he rose into the air like an avenging angel.

Instinctively Toby shot out a pair of fireballs, but this time Tempest was ready. A shimmering blue energy shield blossomed from his small replacement wristband - only about the size of a dustbin lid, but big enough to deflect the two fireballs aside.

'Game's up, Tempest!' shouted Toby, ready to fire another volley. 'I came here for my mother, now hand her over!'

'Of course, I bring all my prisoners out on my heists. Have a picnic; get to know them better,' he said sarcastically. 'She is not here, you imbecile!'

'Then tell me where she is, and I won't have to, say... blow your foot off?'

'Really?' said Doc Tempest smiling. 'You and whose army?'

Pete had had enough. Gritting his teeth he squinted hard at Tempest. The duel laser beams struck his energy shield, shattering a segment away as though it was made of glass. Tempest was surprised. Pete remembered to blink before he cut off his *own* feet.

Toby seized the opportunity and flicked a single fireball at Tempest. It hit his chest, knocking him back down onto the carrier deck.

Both boys zoomed over Tempest who was flat on his back, a sizzling hole in his costume revealing chalky skin beneath. They landed beside him. Toby stalked menacingly towards the villain. Tempest's men were still looting the bank and had not yet noticed their fallen leader.

'Now talk!' shouted Toby through gritted teeth. 'Where

is my mum?'

'My... my base...'

BLAM! Toby fired a flaming ball against the deck, close enough to Tempest's head to singe his hair.

'Not good enough! Where?' persisted Toby.

'Antarctica!' spat Tempest. 'But you won't be going there.'

A shadow fell across the deck. Both boys saw the second barge had positioned itself close to theirs, bow facing them so they had a close up view of the gun turret aimed directly at them. Using it on them would be like using a cannon on an anthill.

'End of your brief careers as trouble makers, I think,' Tempest jeered, already scrabbling away from the boys. Then he yelled: 'Fire!'

Frozen to the spot, Pete and Toby saw a small flicker of light deep within the gun barrel as the energy cannon charged up—

But then the barge shuddered violently. Everybody watched in amazement as a silver streak erupted from its side, leaving a gaping hole!

Emily had punctured the prow of the barge, weakening the superstructure so much that it could no longer support the weight of the cannon. The front bow cannon tipped forward then fell from view as the front end of the barge snapped off with a horrendous screech of tearing metal.

With the anti-gravity system severed in two the remainder of the barge plunged like a rock.

Doc Tempest jumped to his feet and ran to the edge of the deck to watch the stricken vessel fall. Emily landed on the deck, the silver sheen covering her melted away, returning her to normal.

'Hi,' she said almost too casually.

Pete looked at her, open mouthed. 'You are... uh, I mean that was incredible!'

'Em! Am I glad to see you! Where's Lorna?' asked Toby, never taking his eyes from Tempest.

'I don't know. I thought she was with you,' said Emily. She glanced at Pete in such a way that he was sure she knew what he had done.

Doc Tempest turned to face the trio, anger etched on his face. 'You will pay for that!'

'Sue me!' said Pete, suddenly feeling angry.

A sudden chorus of guns click-clacking made the three heroes look up. The rest of the Henchmen had finally stopped looting the gold and rushed over to help their boss. About thirty glyder-discs hovered around them. Thirty resin-rifles pointed in their direction.

'I'd rather take my pound of flesh! Or turn you into ice sculptures' Tempest growled.

The next set of events seemed to happen in slow motion. Emily took several steps forward, chrome slivers already forming across her slight frame.

BLAM! Thirty guns erupted as one.

A mass of glue-bullets headed straight for them. Toby and Pete just had time to raise their hands as if that feeble attempt would stop the barrage.

Half dozen bullets clobbered Emily, the impact propelling her against the wall of gold as the gummy resin swelled on impact with her body.

The remaining shots were aimed at Toby and Pete, but they never reached their target. Instead the bullets seemed to strike an invisible shield in front of the boys, taking the full brunt of the assault.

Real-time seemed to have caught up. Toby and Pete powered into the air, mustering all the speed they could. Below, the glue-bullets had adhered Emily firmly against the gold stacks. It was clear she was going nowhere.

'We've got to go!' urged Pete.

'We can't leave Emily. And where's Lorna?'

Pete licked his dry lips. 'Tobe... mate.' Now was not the right time for explanations. 'We *have* to go!'

Toby allowed Pete to pull him towards the edge of the hurricane wall before they turned around; thirty glyders were in hot pursuit.

'Come on!' screamed Pete.

'We can't leave them!'

'If they've been caught then it's up to *us* to get your mother! There's no way we can beat all those guys on our own! Not right now!'

Tempest's soldiers were gaining ground fast. They would be back in firing range shortly.

Toby was paralysed with indecision. Pete grabbed his friend's shoulder, so hard it hurt Toby.

'Listen to me. They're more use to Tempest alive than dead if he knows we're still around!'

That made some fractured sense to Toby.

'They're catching up!' persisted Pete. Several bullets whooshed past as if to emphasise his point.

Toby cast one last look at the barge where Emily was stuck fast. He wondered where his sister was. More bullets zipped past, forcing them both to fly through the hurricane wall. By the time the pursuing thugs had followed them through the fierce winds the sky was empty.

There was nothing but the echo of a double thunderclap.

TO THE RESCUE_

ANGER MUDDLED TOBY'S MIND, making any rational
thought slip away. They had arrived back at Pete's house,
appearing in his garden amid a heavy shower of rain that had
done little to lift their spirits.

Inside, Toby was ignoring Pete's pleas to stop pacing the
floor. Before they had disappeared through the turbulent
hurricane wall, Toby claimed he saw the distant figure of
Doc Tempest bearing down on Emily who was caught like a
fly in a web. She was struggling, which was a healthy indication she too was alive.

For now.

But what about Lorna?

Pete had excused himself and rummaged through his
room to find his second pair of glasses, the free ones with the
thick frames. Then he spent a harrowing thirty minutes in
the bathroom, replaying the events at Fort Knox over-and-
over. Lorna had swooped into his line of fire... had he hit her?
Or had she been caught in the explosion? It was impossible

to say. But what should he tell Toby? That Lorna might be dead, but it wasn't his fault? It had been an accident?

But that didn't stop him from feeling remorse. He stared at his own pale reflection in the mirror. If he didn't own up then was he as bad a villain? And if he told Toby he thought he'd killed Lorna, would that surely destroy Toby's confidence about finding his mother and Emily? As bad as he felt, Pete thought it would be better to suffer alone. Thinking his sister was missing was bad enough for Toby. Thinking she might be dead was too much.

Toby felt hollow inside. First he'd lost his mother, and now his sister and Emily. He regretted all those pointless arguments he'd had with them... even if it seemed *they* had, mostly, started them. Worse still, he had never told them how much he really did love them, and the opportunity to do so seemed to be fading with each passing minute. If the four of them hadn't been able to stop Doc Tempest, what could two of them do?

Pete nudged his friend out of his stupor and thrust a hot cup of coffee in his hands. 'That'll keep you awake.'

'Yeah, like I need it. I haven't slept properly since all of this started.' Toby stared at the dark brown liquid in the cup and winced. It tasted terrible. 'It's like finding that website was a curse.'

Pete didn't reply. He had no doubts at all about the value of their discovery. 'Look at it this way,' said Pete thoughtfully. 'We didn't get to use *all* of our powers against him.'

'So? We did nothing! We didn't get my mum, we didn't stop the raid and to top it off, we lost Lorna and Emily!'

The mention of Lorna made Pete's cheeks burn red. 'But *they* didn't get to use everything they downloaded either!'

Toby thought about that. There had seemed to be more

than enough Heroic points after Mr Patel had paid them, so they'd greedily clicked on the mouse button, scooping up every icon that appealed to them. Lorna had explained that by downloading multiple powers the chances would be low that they would download completely useless one; if they had several then *one* of them had to be practical.

Only afterwards had Emily wondered what they'd do if there were side effects to possessing so many powers at once. This had caused Pete to tread carefully as they left the house, worried that he might explode at any moment. This train of thought nudged something in the back of Toby's mind.

'They can teleport!'

'So?'

'If they can still teleport, then why don't they just get out of... where ever it is they are and come home?'

Pete was about to say, '*Maybe they can't*', and confess his fears, but stopped himself. 'They could have found something interesting and got distracted, or maybe only one of them has been captured and the other doesn't want to leave... or maybe they found your mum already?'

'Or maybe they're dead,' finished Toby darkly.

A minute's silence passed between them, Toby deep in thought, Pete in an agony of guilt. Finally Pete summoned the courage to speak again.

'Look, it's only been about an hour since we were there. Chances are that Tempest hasn't even returned to his secret base! Besides, you know how difficult these powers are to control?'

Toby slid the cup onto the table, and cradled his head in his hands. He felt miserable.

'We have to think this through,' said Pete regarding his friend sympathetically.

'What do you mean?'

'Well, we still have powers. We've got them for the whole day.' One of the advantages of them paying for the powers was the time they could retain them, in addition to the greater choice on offer.

'Which means we can still save your mom and Emie,' said Pete with conviction.

'And Lorn.'

'Mmm, yeah.'

Toby looked up sharply and Pete felt his stomach churn. Then he noticed that Toby was almost wearing a smile. '*Emie?*'

Pete looked quickly away. 'Shut up.' Finding the website had given Pete a confidence he had been lacking. In private he had flexed his muscles in the mirror, and he was sure there was a *slight* twitch in his biceps.

Toby's thoughts turned black again. 'Do you realize just how big Antarctica is?' He thrust himself back in the chair.

'Yes, it's a continent,' retorted Pete. 'But are you forgetting we have this?'

With a flourish, he placed Tempest's broken command wristband on the table. Toby didn't move, but his eyes fixed on it.

'Have you found out how to use it properly?'

Pete looked away, prodding the device with his finger. 'No... but parts of it work.' He strapped it to his wrist and the screen immediately lit up. He held it up to show Toby the cracked display. It simply showed an arrow - with the words 'SUPPLY CONVOY LOADING'.

'What use is that? What does it even mean?'

Pete flicked on the television in the kitchen. The News was reporting on the hurricane that had just decimated Fort

Knox, and a Whitehouse spokesman was assuring a press conference that it was just a weather abnormality and the Federal U.S. gold reserves were still perfectly intact.

'That's right, intact in somebody else's pocket now,' mumbled Toby.

The Whitehouse spokesman skilfully spun the press conference towards the threat of global warming, and away from the fact that the country was almost bankrupt.

The news report switched to a confused meteorologist who stood in front of a giant satellite image of the storm.

'Now the weather system has performed an extraordinary U-turn and is heading out to sea at an incredible speed... I've never seen anything like this before!' Toby straightened up in his chair. He glanced at Pete who was also listening intently. The weather woman continued as computer graphics overlaid the hurricane with speeds and wind directions.

'The storm must be trapped in an atmospheric super jet stream. Over land the winds have died almost to nothing as the storm passed back into the Gulf of Mexico. Although ground damage is high - never before has a storm moved with such speed - at this time official estimates are...'

The woman hesitated onscreen as she read the autocue that rolled invisibly across the camera. To Toby and Pete it looked like she was starring right at them. 'A thousand miles per hour and increasing? Of course that is impossible—'

Pete knocked the television off. Toby threw him an angry glance.

'Hey! I was watching that!'

'No, you were feeling sorry for yourself! Think! We're heroes! Heroes have good times and bad times - but they don't sulk about it.' He waved a comic for emphasis.

Toby shook his head. 'So the storm's gone! We know he's headed back to a base somewhere in Antarctica - but that still doesn't help us! I bet he'll be there by now!'

Pete sighed, but said nothing. Instead he stared at the wristband. *If only it worked properly*, he thought, *we could have maybe figured out a way to track Tempest down—*

The arrow on the wristband's screen pointed over Toby's left shoulder. Pete frowned. 'The arrow's pointing that way.'

'Are you trying to tell me that Doc Tempest's secret base is in your kitchen?' Toby quipped.

Pete said nothing. Instead he turned himself completely around. The arrow remained true, pointing beyond Toby's shoulder. The flicker of a smile started to crack Pete's face. 'It's pointing the way!'

'Huh?'

'The arrow will take us straight to him!' said Pete with a trace of pride over his discovery. 'Whatever the 'supply line' is, it will lead us to Tempest and the others!'

When Toby and Pete had escaped, Doc Tempest had thrown an exhausting tantrum. When he calmed he fell into a sulk and glowered at Emily; at least he had a prisoner. But his temper further exploded when he realized that his other barge was damaged beyond repair and there was still half the gold left in the vault.

The thieves had all grouped together close to the undamaged barge as Doc Tempest manipulated his small wristband, and a giant yellow shimmering shield radiated around his entire fleet, generated by some technical gizmo inside the carrier.

Tempest snarled at his men ordering them to shackle

Emily for now and then imprison her when they arrived back at the base. He gave a disparaging smile, revealing his fang-like teeth, and Emily briefly wondered if he'd ever used a toothbrush on them.

'You're an addition to my insurance plan if those friends of yours try anything again! Now I've got two hostages, I can afford to kill one of you.'

Numerous thoughts swirled through Emily's mind. She was starting to worry that she would never see her family again. Never have the chance to explain about her adventures. She poked the thoughts away. She was an optimist and knew while she was alive there was hope. She refused to show any fear to Doc Tempest.

'Doc Tempest? Doctor of *what* exactly? I doubt you've had any medical training in your life. And how did your head get like that? Maybe *you* should see a doctor?'

With a bark of resentment Tempest stomped off barking orders to his men, presumably to organise getting the stolen gold back to base. While guards had waited for the glue to soften Emily futilely struggled against it. She couldn't get free no matter how much she kept transforming herself into living metal and back, but it was a trick that amused the guards. She knew that her other downloaded powers involved her hands, but as soon as they were free a guard had slapped a solid pair of handcuffs on her wrists and thumbed a four-digit number on the keypad. A light flickered and the cuffs automatically tightened on her wrist. She suddenly felt weak. Try as she might, she could no longer transform herself into the silver bullet.

The squad smirked at her struggles.

'Forget it, darlin,' said one. 'Latest fing the boss got from a pal of 'is. Stops them superpowers so you can't use 'em against me and the lads.'

Emily grunted in frustration but struggled again.

'And if ya thinkin' of tryin' to unlock 'em without that code - forget it. It's me credit card pin number, so you ain't got a chance!'

'Seven-four-one-three is your pin number?' said Emily who had been watching carefully. She knew it was stupid to mention it, but it was worth it to see the smile drop from the thug's face as he quickly looked at his unscrupulous colleagues who could now all use his credit card.

'I'll be changin' that as soon as I gets back!' he said loudly, grabbing Emily's wrists and entering another code, making sure she could not see this time. Then they left her alone.

In the frenetic action she only had time to think for herself. But now she recalled the last time she'd seen Lorna. Emily went white. Pete had blindly been firing laser bolts from his eyes and Lorna had been in the line of fire. The conclusion slammed into place: Pete had shot Lorna!

Emily knew it was an accident. Pete would never hurt anyone. But where was Lorna now? Was she still alive? Hiding somewhere injured? Emily felt tears roll down her cheeks.

The mercenaries had settled at the edge of the carrier deck, talking about sport and discussing what cars they should buy with the cut they'd be getting from this job. They glanced at Emily, and even though the resin had dissolved, didn't seem too bothered to let her walk to the edge of the deck and peer down - anything to take her mind off her over-active imagination.

Beyond the yellow shield, the landscape was moving at such a speed it was a blur. Almost instantly it changed to deep blue, and Emily guessed they were passing over the sea. The force field around them seemed to cancel out any feeling of movement or cold, especially when the blue blur transformed into plain white. Snow, Emily correctly guessed.

After an hour the craft slowed over a hostile mountain range, and they approached an oblong opening cut in the rocky peak like a giant letterbox. They passed into an enormous space where Tempest's soldiers awaited in rows like a well drilled army.

The barge landed in a specially made berth, and Emily was taken away, only glimpsing Doc Tempest again as he stalked in the opposite direction.

Emily was led through a network of corridors sculpted from ice. She completely lost her sense of direction in the twists and turns. They reached another corridor with about ten sets of identical doors either side. The guard escorting her opened one of the smooth metal doors and shoved her inside.

'Enjoy your new home!' he sneered as the door slid closed.

Emily looked around the small, windowless ice room. There was a bed with a single blanket that smelt like a dog had been sleeping on it for a month. She sat down, hoping that help was on its way and hoping that she was wrong about Lorna and that she was safely with Toby and Pete.

Sarah Wilkinson had been roused from a feverish sleep. A thin film of sweat clung to her and she was starting to tremble. She desperately needed her insulin.

A guard escorted her at gunpoint into a small rail-pod. The carriage shot along the track and within a minute they had reached their destination, a circular room that she guessed must be at the apex of the mountain.

Doc Tempest was waiting for her, gazing through a set of panoramic windows. Sarah's planned vitriolic outburst towards her captor died in her throat when she glimpsed the vista beyond the window. Snow blanketed the ground as far as the horizon, the slope of the mountain dipping below her. It was if they were standing on top of the world, but even as she watched, heavy grey clouds discharged snow that was thickening by the instant. Within moments, the grandiose view was replaced by a savage blizzard.

Doc Tempest turned to face her. Sarah was pale, and had refused to eat the gruel she had been served while locked up. Even though she felt weak, she still looked defiant.

Tempest smirked. 'Not feeling so good, eh?'

'I'm diabetic. I need my insulin.'

'Sorry. I'm not *that* kind of doctor. Can't help you there.' He gestured outside. 'Beautiful weather though.'

'I prefer somewhere hot.'

'Very soon you will have a choice, my dear,' said Tempest walking in a wide circle, gently holding his arms behind his back like an army general. 'You can have a searing hot desert, or a frozen winter wasteland. There will be no middle ground if the governments of the world don't bow to my wishes!'

'Why do this? It's madness!'

'Madness? No, it's power! I control the *wever* - and soon I will control the world!'

'Like I said, madness.'

Doc Tempest shot her a look of contempt. 'Any country that refuses to instate me as their leader will fry under a baking sun, or freeze under a snow drift a mile high! Which bit of that plan is mad? I'm just helping nudge things along.'

'That's impossible!'

'Nothing is impossible if you have the motivation and the cash! I've always had he motivation and now I have most of the US Federal reserve. Nothing can go wrong!'

'And what have *I* got to do with this?' demanded Sarah.

'Your brats have been proving troublesome in my plans.'

'My children?'

Doc Tempest wheeled around, raising his finger in warning.

'Don't play stupid with me! It's pointless trying to keep their identities secret. They are a constant nuisance and if they try and interfere *again* I swear I will return you to them... one piece at a time.'

Tempest was obviously crazy if he thought her children were any kind of threat. But the warning had stirred a primeval mothering instinct inside Sarah.

'Listen, bucket-head, I have no idea what you're talking about. My kids are in school. But if you even look at them the wrong way, I will beat you senseless! I'm sure the police are already tracking you down, you freak.'

Doc Tempest grabbed her wrists and Sarah shrieked as an intense chill ran through her arms. She tried to pull away, but was too weak and the villain had a vice-like grip. She watched in horror as frost drifted painfully across her hands.

'Stop!' she whimpered.

Tempest released her, and the warmth slowly trickled back into her hands. He scowled. 'You have been warned!'

Doc Tempest's boots thumped heavily across the floor as he strode away from her, across the command centre.

. . .

Sarah was dragged away, back towards the rail-pod. The guard shoved her inside. The door closed, or rather attempted to close, but opened again.

'Stupid door,' grumbled the guard as he thumbed the button irritably. The pod door swished closed on the second attempt.

Sarah sensed the acceleration, and soon they were shooting around the edge of the mountain again. She vigorously rubbed her wrists and she shivered as she recalled the sensation of her blood freezing in her veins. She was completely baffled by that last conversation. Her children? What have her children got to do with this monster?

She didn't have time to muse for long. The rail-pod pulled up and the door slid open - then the guard did a very strange thing.

He raised his rifle in front of him with a confused expression, shook it, then forced the butt of the weapon against his own face so hard that he was lifted off his feet and fell against the wall of the pod where he lay unconscious.

Sarah looked around, bewildered, but not for long. She was alone, with the sudden possibility of escape.

Using all her strength she dragged the unconscious guard from the pod and took his resin-rifle. She stepped back inside the pod, slumped on the seat and thumbed the button, hoping it would take her to freedom.

The temperature had plummeted as Toby and Pete flew south, arms extended to streamline themselves and increase their speed. They couldn't teleport, as they had no idea of exactly *where* they were going, so they had reluctantly flown.

Pete thought they were going faster than sound, and silently wondered if it would still be possible to talk.

The silent flight had them both lost in thought. Toby was imagining a fond reunion with his mother and Lorna. But how long could she last without her medication? For reassurance he touched his pocket that held his mother's insulin kit. When he thought of Lorna he felt rotten for suppressing her desire to use the powers to gain some fame. Maybe if he had just let her then she wouldn't be missing now? Perhaps none of them would be in this mess.

Pete was battling his guilt. He kept repeating that it was an accident. He tried to persuade himself that it was Lorna's fault for getting in his way - but he couldn't. And when he was thinking about Lorna, he was feeling sick because he had let Tempest's gold slip through his fingers... what other good things would he have to miss out on? Before the flight was halfway over, he'd convinced himself that accepting Tempest's offer would have made him feel less guilty over what happened to Lorna.

Pete and Toby had been following the direction indicated by the arrow for almost three hours, and now the light was fading. Already they both agreed they should have worn warmer clothing, especially when they knew their ultimate destination would be supremely cold.

For some time they had been over water, so there was no discernible sense of progression, aside from a plump full moon that slowly glided across the sky ahead of them. Lights appeared on the horizon, marking a small island. Within minutes they zipped past the island, and Pete drew himself up in a wide arc, studying the wristband. Toby followed his friend as he doubled back. Pete pointed to the device excitedly.

'It's here! The arrow's pointing here!' The arrow on the display revolved so it was constantly pointing towards the landmass.

Toby felt his hopes rise. 'Let's go down... but be careful!'

Closer inspection of the island revealed it to be nothing more than a clump of barren mountains and long-extinct volcanoes, inaccessible from the sea. A wide plateau offered enough room for a long landing strip and several large hangars. They could see people walking around the back of a large Hercules transport plane that sat on the runway. Fork-lift trucks were loading square supply pallets under the harsh glare of floodlights.

Toby and Pete landed on a slope that offered a clear view of the proceedings.

'The supply link,' whispered Pete. 'Doc Tempest and his men have to eat. This is where they ship it all in.'

Toby nodded. 'So these planes are carrying supplies straight to him! All we have to do is stow away onboard and they'll take us to his secret base. Come on!'

Toby jumped to his feet and scrambled down the slope. Black scree rolled underfoot and made it tough going, and he almost lost his balance on more than one occasion. He kept to the shadows so as not to be seen.

When he reached the flat concrete surface of the plateau, Pete was already there, shaking his head.

'It was easier flying down!'

They were close to one of the five big hangars situated at the end of the runway. The hangar directly across from them contained another Hercules, the engines were surrounded with scaffolding, and maintenance crews were tinkering with the various gears and electronics. The closest hangar had rows of wooden pallets, some standing as tall as the boys, covered in canvas webbing to hold them together; others were being built up a box at a time by ground crews wearing the familiar grey uniform. Luckily the crews were at the far end of the hangar, which was as wide as a football field is long.

'Looks like there's room for a couple more pallets, then I reckon it'll take off,' said Toby. 'Can't see any signs of a pilot though.'

He turned to Pete, but discovered he had been talking to himself. Pete had crept forward on all fours to one of the half-built pallets and was tearing a box open.

'Pete!' Toby hissed, terrified his voice would be overheard. But it seemed that not even Pete could hear him.

Pete pulled something out of the box and held it up for Toby to see, giving the thumbs-up with his other hand. It was thermal protection gear, exactly what was needed if they were travelling to the icy wastes of Antarctica.

They had to open several boxes to find something approximating their size. Obviously Doc Tempest had a penchant for hiring only tall people. But after five minutes of rummaging they had located long-sleeved tops, complete with gloves, and trousers with built in socks. It was all made out of a thin material like a wetsuit, but it offered much greater insulation and it all fitted nicely under their jeans and t-shirts. They also found thicker, thermal coats with fur-lined hoods. The multiple layers would certainly keep them warm in the coldest place on earth.

They'd hidden behind a tall stack of boxes as they plundered the supplies, but had been oblivious to how much noise or mess they were creating as they tore open the plastic wrapping the clothes came in.

'Wot you doin' 'ere?' snarled a deep voice.

A gorilla of a man stood over them. Pete was balanced on one foot and so toppled over in surprise. Toby hesitated.

'Er...quality inspection?'

The huge man punched a fist into his open palm. His hands were the size of plates. 'Finks we 'ave trespassers!' the gorilla rumbled. He leaned down and grabbed Pete by the scruff of his jacket. Pete's feet pedalled helplessly as he was hoisted up.

'Let him go!' growled Toby.

The man turned his enormous head towards Toby and grinned, showing tombstone-like teeth. 'Or wot?'

A good question, thought Toby. Hurling a fireball at the man seemed a little extreme, and he didn't have time to experiment to find out what other power he'd downloaded.

Instead, he threw a punch. Toby knew it would be like hitting an elephant, but he had to try *something*. His fist arced towards the man's flabby stomach. Toby watched in astonishment as his hand grew larger, his fingers swelling into fat sausages then bigger still. By the time his hand had connected with the thug's stomach it was three times larger than normal.

And much more devastating.

The goon dropped Pete, and crumpled over as Toby slugged him in the gut. The giant fist propelled him three meters across the hangar before he slammed into a shelving unit and was buried under a mound of heavy boxes that knocked him out cold.

Toby stared at his hand. It rapidly shrank back to normal.

'Wow,' said Pete. 'Can you do that with the rest of your body?'

Luckily nobody paid too much attention to the falling boxes across the other side of the hangar. Had they bothered to investigate, the work crew knew a supervisor would only have ordered them to clean it up. It was less effort to turn a blind eye to somebody's bad stacking. They didn't see the two boys race across the hangar and climb on top of the pallet nearest the door. It was a plan concocted at the spur of the moment by Toby, and seemed to be the easiest way onto the aircraft. They lay flat, the whole pallet rocking as the forklift scooped it up. The boys were carried across the runway and up the loading ramp of the Hercules.

They waited as technicians secured the pallet with straps so it wouldn't shift during flight. Receding footsteps down the ramp indicated the boys were alone. But they waited for the loud rumble of the cargo door to automatically close before they clambered from their hiding place.

Several dim recessed ceiling lights lit the hold. All of the available floor space was taken up with supply pallets. They clambered over the boxes; at the front of the cargo hold were two grubby and frayed, padded chairs bolted to the wall, facing the wrong way like those used by airline stewards.

Between the seats was a door that was open a crack. It led to the cockpit. Toby placed his finger over his lips to silence Pete, who was about to speak. If the pilot caught them now, their plan would be ruined.

Toby edged forward and peered through the gap into the cockpit, as they felt the four powerful turboprop engines vibrate to life with a deep rumble. His brow furrowed; there was no pilot. Instead, a grey box was bolted onto the control panel, dozens of wires curling from it and into the controls, physically hacking the flight system. The whole appearance was, well, makeshift.

'Looks like they're remotely flying the plane!'

Pete gaped, and pushed forward to have a look. He came away somewhat disappointed.

'So we're one big drone. You know, with all that money he's stolen, you'd expect Tempest to build something cool. This looks like a load of junk welded together!'

The cockpit door suddenly slammed shut, locking automatically with solid cross spars. Pete tried to open it, but it wouldn't budge. Before he could try anything else, the plane rocked as it started to taxi.

'Better strap in quickly!' shouted Toby.

They dashed into the jump seats as the aircraft taxied across the runway and took position. They just managed to strap themselves in as the plane jounced forward, thrusting them forcibly against their harnesses. Taking off backwards was most definitely a different experience.

The Hercules transport plane rose so steeply that if they hadn't strapped themselves in, they would have fallen to the back of the fuselage.

When the plane finally levelled they allowed themselves to relax. Eventually Pete nodded off, snoring deeply. Toby slumbered uneasily, even though the last few nights were catching up on him, making him feel weak. He was worried about his mother, Lorna and Emily. He hoped they were safe and sound, but he knew they were in grave danger.

THE STORM ENGINE_

Doc Tempest sat behind a desk, in front of a high-definition video camera. The man behind the camera had once worked in the fashion business, and hated the black and grey uniform he was made to wear. But he didn't complain. This job paid much more, and he had the responsibility of coordinating the ransom demands. Right now he was trying to convince the maniacal supervillain before him to put on a little makeup.

'NO!' bellowed Tempest.

'But... your skin,' stammered the man in his Spanish accent. 'Your skin is so greasy. It reflects the light like a mirror!'

'It's supposed to be greasy! I'm supposed to look menacing!'

The other technicians in the command centre tactfully avoided looking across, and instead they intently studied the computer screens that controlled every aspect of the base.

'Okay, okay... when you're ready then.'

The Spaniard switched on the camera and folded his arms expectantly. Doc Tempest glowered across the table.

'My name is Doc Tempest, and already you have seen the awesome power of my *wever* machine. And I—'

'Stop! Stop!' screamed the man, pausing the camera.

'What?' fumed Tempest. 'I was in mid-flow, you idiot!'

'You said *wever*… not weather… you missed the '*th*'.'

Tempest's eyes burned furiously. 'I did *not*.'

'Did too, and it didn't sound menacing *at all*.'

Doc Tempest sucked in his breath and ran his tongue over his pointed teeth. He hated them and was sure they added a lisp to his voice, and when he bit his tongue, it was sheer agony. But he said nothing. He nodded and twirled his finger to indicate the camera should be started again.

'Action,' piped the cameraman after he had pressed the button.

'My name is *Doc Tempest*,' he slammed his fist against the desk for emphasis with such force the vibrations made the camera tip over. The cameraman lunged for it, catching it just before it hit the floor.

'Don't do that!'

'Keep rolling!' shouted Tempest, as the cameraman levelled the tripod.

'My name is—'

A high-pitched beep suddenly rose from the control panel, completely throwing Tempest. He jumped to his feet, clenched his fist and punched the air towards the camera-man. A blazing white beam enveloped the Spaniard who barely had time to raise his arms. When the light died everybody could see he was covered in a glistening frost, literally frozen on the spot.

Doc Tempest spun around and glared at his technicians. '*What* is that alarm?'

'It's the airborne radar, it has detected one of the scheduled transport aircraft.'

'So? It's supposed to be here.'

'Ah... but it's detected two life forms onboard. Definitely human, and there's supposed to be nothing but supplies.'

Tempest strode over to the terminal and studied the radar screen. It showed black swirling storm clouds, and one solid inbound blip that was identified as a C-130 Hercules Transport.

'People?'

'I radioed the depot. They said they didn't put anybody onboard. It's unauthorized.'

Doc Tempest glared at the screen. 'It's *them*, trying to sneak in on a rescue mission, no less.'

'What shall we do?'

'Blow them out of the sky.'

Tempest thumbed a button that activated the drinks dispenser. He sighed, he really would have to have a word with the Council of Evil electricians who had labelled everything incorrectly.

He thumbed another button and activated the missile defence system.

Across the frozen wastes, a mound of snow cracked, then chunks fell away as the missile launcher buried beneath spun to life. The hydraulic rig twisted the four Patriot missiles skyward, tracking the aircraft hidden in the dense clouds. The radar had locked onto the heat-signature of the Hercules' portside engines.

The exhaust of the missile flared to life, and it shot into the sky. There's no way it could miss its target.

The Hercules shimmied as the violent blizzard shook it. Pete gripped his harness tightly. Even if he had superpowers he felt safer holding onto something solid. His sleep had been troubled by a dream in which he saw Lorna pointing an accusing finger at him and he had woken up with a yelp.

'Reckon we must nearly be there,' said Toby. 'Air temperature's really dropped.'

Pete licked his dry lips and plucked up the courage to speak. 'Tobe... there's something I need to tell you.'

Toby frowned. With the danger they were in, now was not the time for confessions or complaints.

'It's about Lorna. I... I sho—'

Tempest's missile chose that moment to slam into a port side engine and words were snatched from Pete's mouth as the aircraft dropped from the sky.

Emily looked up as her cell door slid open and tensed herself, ready for anything.

Nobody was there.

She edged into the corridor. It was empty.

'Hello?'

The air suddenly shimmered right in front of her; it looked like a heat-haze but resolved itself in to a familiar face that was beaming from ear-to-ear.

'Lorna!' exclaimed Emily, hugging her friend tightly. 'You're alive! How did you manage that? I thought Pete had... had...'

'Remember I clicked on that blank button on the website and we thought it wasn't a real option? It turns out it was invisibility! When Pete blew up that glyder, I just managed to get out of the way but got such a fright that it triggered the power.'

Emily shook her head, relieved that she was wrong about Pete.

'I fought Tempest alongside you and I was in front of my brother when those thugs fired their resin-rifles. That saved him and Pete from getting caught. Luckily nobody thought to check the other glue pile. That was me in there.'

'So you followed me in?'

'I watched where they put you.' Lorna looked apologetic. 'I didn't free you because I thought that might trigger some alarms and I needed to explore the base.'

'I would have done the same. What did you discover?'

'I found out Doc Tempest is using weather control to blackmail governments so he can take over entire countries. And I found my mum!'

'Is she okay?'

'She's weak and needs her insulin, but at least she's still able to walk. Of course she couldn't see me, and I didn't want to just talk to her. I mean, hearing a voice talking to you from thin air is spooky. And I suddenly realized that if she saw me then I'd have to explain us all being here. She'd *know* our secret.'

'I hadn't thought of that. So how are we going to get her out without her knowing it's us?'

'I have no idea. But I freed her, so she's wandering around here somewhere. She was kept on a different level from you. I thought I better get you next.'

'Thanks, but I still have these things,' said Emily holding up her shackled wrists.

'Ah, time for my other power. Hold your hands out.'

Emily extended her arms as far as possible. Lorna held her hand out, fingers rigid, like a karate pose. Then her hands started to glow white-hot.

'I've never actually seen this before!' cried Lorna excitedly. 'I was invisible every other time!'

She struck down, easily severing Emily's handcuffs; the metal bubbled from the heat. Emily shook them off, rubbing life back into her wrists. Lorna blew on her hands, the heat suddenly vanishing.

'There you go!'

'Nice trick,' agreed Emily. 'Now let's get your mum and get out of here.'

She took a step forward, but Lorna grabbed her arm and pulled her back. 'It's not going to be that easy.'

'Why not?'

'We only have a few hours left with these powers. We don't want mum to know about them. And we can't leave Tempest to carry out the rest of his plan. He's crazy enough to destroy the world!'

'So you're saying we have to stop all of this on our own?'

'We won't be on our own. If I know my brother he'll probably already be here, causing chaos as usual!'

Toby stumbled in the snow, falling flat on his face. He was weak from both grief and lack of sleep. The missiles had struck the Hercules and they had crashed into the mountainside. The last he saw of Pete was when the burning fuselage raced down the slope towards them. He wondered what Pete was trying to tell him before the missile hit. Toby forced himself to cling on to the reason they had come to this inhospitable wilderness, to find Lorna and rescue his mother and Emily.

He picked himself up, his clothes so white with frost he almost blended into the landscape. Through the blizzard he could just see the rest of the towering peaks of the Antarctic's Neptune Range, in particular one that had a pair of flashing beacons indicating the entrance to a hangar. That *had* to be Doc Tempest's lair.

The only problem was, it was going to be a *long* climb.

'You know, Toby,' said a voice. 'You always have to do things the hard way.'

Toby blinked the snow from his eyes... and looked up. Pete was hovering just above him.

'Pete? You're alive!'

'Of course I am! Unlike you, I keep remembering that I can *fly*! Why are you walking, you idiot? After Tempest's hurricane, these winds aren't so bad.'

Toby started to shake with relief. The fatigue he had been feeling dropped from his shoulders and he suddenly felt he could go for hours without stopping. He jumped into the air and hovered next to his best mate.

'You have no idea how glad I am to see you!' he said.

'Toby, I need to tell you something.'

Toby shook his head. 'No, tell me after all this is over. We're so close to rescuing them now. That's what's important.'

Pete took a deep breath and nodded. 'Okay. You're right. Now let's go and be heroes!'

. . .

Footsteps echoed down the ice corridor. Sarah stopped and tensed as the footsteps continued, getting louder as they approached. A quick check confirmed that there were no hiding places in the corridor, and it was much too far to turn and run back the way she had come in order to hide around the corner. Instead she raised the rifle she had taken, and aimed it like she had seen in so many movies. The barrel trembled in her weakened state.

A guard turned the corner, his nose buried in a comic as he walked. He changed direction automatically, only looking up at the last moment to see the business end of a resin-rifle pointing right at him.

'This is your unlucky day,' Sarah said through gritted her teeth, and then she fired. There was no recoil in the weapon, just a hiss of gas as three black, sticky globules shot out striking the man across the mouth and chest and crumpling his comic. He staggered backwards as the glue-balls expanded, fastening against the wall.

Sarah examined her handiwork with satisfaction. 'Oops,' she said with a smile as she passed him. She was unsure where she found the energy to keep walking. She had to get some sugar, and fast. It was only a matter of time before she became hypoglycaemic and passed out. She decided to try and find a canteen. All these people had to eat, and if there was food, there would be sugar. Without her insulin that was her only hope.

She forced herself to continue down the stark corridor, and praised herself on handling the unreal situation so well. She had finally accepted that his wasn't a hallucination bought on by her illness. First a tornado struck her house, created by a villain who kidnapped her; then she was brought to a secret ice base where a bunch of would be saviours *flew* through the air. Then the freaky-headed kidnapper had warned that her children should not try to rescue her. And despite the odds, she had managed to escape.

It was notably warmer. Sarah slowed her pace as a set of sliding double-doors became visible ahead. She approached cautiously, rifle poised, ears straining against the silence. The doors slid open as she got close and a warm red glow emanated from within. Curious, Sarah edged closer and peered around the corner.

She had a view from a balcony at the top of the spacious room, overlooking a transparent cylinder that was as wide as a street and six storeys high. Metallic rings were set along the tube at regular intervals and a red pulse of energy occasionally shot up the column.

Sneaking a look below, Sarah could see half a dozen technicians casually walking between control panels that were linked to the column by thick cables. She guessed it was an electrical generator. But it was huge and she wondered what kind of device required such power?

Without warning a sound wave shook her ribs. It had come from the energy column as it flared brighter. The pulses within the transparent surface gained frequency.

Sarah had the sneaking suspicion that the generator was powering up.

Lorna's sense of direction was far superior to her brother's, but even so she was lost. They had encountered several henchmen walking around the complex and had dealt with them using their combined powers. It was so easy, Lorna almost felt sorry for them.

'I thought you knew the way out?' said Emily. She was sure they had walked down this particular stretch of corridor before.

'Me too.'

'And if we can't even find the way out, how are we going to find your mother again?'

Lorna felt a bit annoyed. She had just rescued her friend, but all Emily had done was complain they were lost. 'We haven't heard any sirens so far, so I think it's safe to assume they don't know she's escaped.'

'Does this corridor seemed sloped to you? It feels like we've been climbing upwards.'

Lorna didn't reply, but inwardly she agreed, they could well be near the top of the mountain by now.

Lorna suddenly stopped and Emily bumped into her. 'What's—?'

'Sssh,' said Lorna, putting her finger over her lips, making more noise than Emily had been. 'Listen!'

Emily couldn't hear anything, and for a moment thought Lorna must have downloaded super-hearing or something. But then she caught it: the faintest sounds of activity, punctuated by the distinct crackle of a monotonous voice over a public address system. It sounded just like a distant railway station.

'The hangar!' said Lorna excitedly as she took off in the direction of the noise. 'I knew we weren't lost!'

But it wasn't the hangar. It was another cavernous room, but this one was circular, almost like—

'We're at the peak of the mountain!' exclaimed Emily in a whisper.

The mountains peak had been removed and replaced with a wide glass dome, supported by steel spars and massive pneumatic rams. It looked as though the top of the mountain could be opened on a hinge. The room was bustling with lab-coated scientists who examined multiple computer banks. The whole setup reminded Lorna of sequences she had seen on television of NASA Mission Command, except in the centre of this room was an intricate device.

It resembled a giant gun, like the ones that had been mounted on the front of Doc Tempest's flying barges. Except this was longer, with a small satellite dish attached to the tip of the barrel. The machine had angular fins, like a shark, and concentric, transparent rings dispersed along the barrel which moved closer together or further apart as the technicians ran a series of diagnostic checks on the machine.

Emily and Lorna entered the room and hid behind a bank of wooden packing crates against the wall. Most were empty, but some had spare parts inside, nestled in shredded newspaper. Emily opened her mouth to say something, but there was no sign of Lorna.

'Lorn?' she whispered. A slight pressure to her shoulder startled Emily, but she quickly realized Lorna had made herself invisible so she could stand up for a better view.

A small knot of technicians gathered around a computer screen, their voices carrying across the room. 'Extend the dampening plane by forty degrees!' As if in answer, the concentric rings along the barrel spaced further apart with a high-pitch whine of motors, similar to a dentist drill.

'Rotate the gimbal a hundred and ten along the x-axis, and increase electron flow by twenty percent,' said another technician who seemed to be in charge. 'We've finally got our coordinates: Washington D.C.'

A cheer went up. The entire gun rotated around on a

complex arrangement of gears and hydraulics, angling the dish at the end of the weapon in a subtly different direction.

'Storm Engine primed!' shouted another technician. 'Let's see how those suits in Washington like a rain of electrical fire!' Chuckles filled the room. 'Just hope the bossman gives the nod soon, I'm starving! What time's the canteen close?'

Invisible fingers tugged Emily's arm, and she allowed herself to be pulled from the room by Lorna. It was a freaky experience watching her own arm lead her from the room.

They moved further down the corridor, which offered cover behind yet more stacked supply crates. The air shimmered as Lorna became visible.

'That's Doc Tempest's weather machine! That's how he's been able to create those storms!'

Emily nodded. 'And it sounds like Washington is going to be burnt off the map. We have to find a way of stopping it!'

'We also have to find our way out of here. The moment we try and sabotage that weapon, they'll know we're here. I have to get my mum out first.'

Emily sighed. 'It still doesn't change the fact that we don't know where the hangar is.'

'Hey!' The voice made them turn - a guard was staring at them, rifle levelled, his finger on the trigger. Lorna and Emily froze like rabbits caught in headlights, raising their hands in surrender. 'Don't try anything funny or you'll know about it!'

'No!' whimpered Emily. They had been so close to success; to get caught just as they rescued Lorna's mother didn't seem fair. The man stared hard at her.

'No!' the man repeated.

'I'm not doing anything!' said Emily in alarm. Her body

save space. Pete took some satisfaction in noticing there were many empty slots. Testament to the heroes' combined might.

'So many doors,' said Toby looking around. 'Which one is the right one?'

'Assuming they're all being held together. We need some kind of map,' said Pete. 'Maybe they have one of those maps on the wall with a dot saying, "You Are Here"?'

'Somehow, I doubt it. And if we get lost, this will turn into one rubbish rescue!'

'I don't think that's going to be too much of a problem,' said Pete.

Toby shook his head. Sometimes Pete was just too over-optimistic. He turned to his friend.

'That *is* your mum, right?' Pete said, pointing.

Toby's head snapped around. His mother had appeared from a passageway at the back of the hangar. She looked weak and dishevelled and was clutching a rifle. She stumbled behind a stack of barrels and was clearly in need of her medication.

'Wow, she's got a gun!' said Pete, stating the obvious. 'I didn't know your mum was so adventurous!'

Neither did Toby. His hand fell onto to diabetes kit stashed in his pocket. He was about to comment, relief coursing through him, when movement across on the mezzanine level caught his attention; Lorna and Emily ran from an opposite corridor and paused to take in the hangar. Once more his heart leapt, and he heard Pete gasp as he spotted them too.

'Lorna! She's alive!'

Tears of joy welled in Pete's eyes and he almost fell down in relief. Nobody had seen the boys hovering in the shadows of the hangar corner, but Lorna and Emily had spotted

Sarah. With complete disregard for their own safety, they jumped from the mezzanine and glided down in front of Sarah, who yelped loudly in surprise.

Even from this distance, Toby could see the astonishment and joy etched on his mother's face as she hugged Lorna tightly. Toby felt an unexpected surge of jealousy. His mum would never hug him like that.

But that feeling vaporised when he noticed a group of guards advancing towards his mother's hiding place. They must have heard her loud yelp of surprise.

Worse still, Sarah, Emily and Lorna hadn't seen them approaching.

ONCE SARAH HAD CRUSHED the breath from Lorna in a mighty hug, she held her daughter at arm's length and studied her up and down.

'What are you doing here? Did that nutter kidnap you too?' Then she noticed Emily was with her. 'Emily? What—?'

'There's no time to explain, mum. We're here to rescue you!'

Sarah was flabbergasted. This was too much to take in. She adopted her stern parental tone. 'I may be feeling awful but there's always time to explain, young lady!'

'Yeah, please explain,' said a deep male voice. They all turned to see ten armed soldiers surrounding them. 'Because I think this is the end of your little super-rescue attempt.'

Lorna noticed something behind Tempest's soldiers. She replied with a smile: 'No. This is only the beginning.'

The lead guard was puzzled for a second, a witty reply formulating in his mind. But before he could utter it a series of fireballs exploded into the barrels around them. The men scattered as the fuel drums exploded vertically into the air like rockets.

Lorna and Emily pulled Sarah back from the conflagration just as a pair of laser beams raked across the floor, severing three of the thugs' weapons. Everybody craned around to see—

'Toby!' exclaimed Sarah in surprise. 'What are you doing... flying?' she finished lamely.

The boys dropped down and Toby handed his mother the insulin.

'Quick, mum, take it.'

Relief flooded across Lorna's face then she was surprised when Pete hugged her slightly.

'Thank God you're okay! I thought I'd killed you!'

Toby looked surprised, but Lorna succeeded in pushing him away with a grin. 'You're not that good a shot!' She winked at her brother. 'Good to see you again! I knew you wouldn't leave us'

'You too... I thought...' he hesitated; talking about his feelings was something that didn't come easy. So he finished lamely. 'Never mind.'

Even with trembling fingers it had taken Sarah only moments to inject the insulin into her system. It was not a miracle cure, but already she was feeling the benefits.

Pete smiled at Emily. 'Glad you're okay. Fighting fit?'

'Oh, yeah,' grinned Emily.

Together the four heroes stood in front of Sarah, poised for action. It only took a few seconds for the remaining armed men to rally, and the explosion had already caught the attention of a dozen more who were running their way.

'Get 'em!' yelled Toby.

Several of things happened in the next ten seconds. All

four heroes took to the air. Emily rippled as the chrome-skin enveloped her body.

Lorna became invisible and in the next instant the two closest guards fell; one smashed across the jaw, the other clutching his crotch in agony as the invisible assailant whirled between them.

Pete, his glasses perched on his forehead, swooped low, twin lasers burning from his pupils, striking several troopers down. He was being careful to attack at a close range, which enabled him to positively identify which blur was the enemy.

Toby rocketed straight up, feeling the burning power in his hands swell with a ferocity he hadn't experienced before. Once he reached the ceiling he pointed downwards, unleashing countless fireballs from his crackling fingertips. They smashed into the ground, scattering men and exploding equipment.

Sarah watched in total disbelief. A hand on her shoulder brought her crashing back to reality. She cocked her head to see a serious looking mercenary behind. Even in her weakened condition she rifle-butted him firmly in his face. He fell to the floor, visor cracked, blood running from his nose and spitting teeth.

Lorna hurtled through a dozen soldiers, all of who ricocheted from her solid mass like pins struck with a bowling ball. She gained some height, in time to see several more goons advancing on Sarah; but they fell from invisible blows.

The air was suddenly filled with glue-bullets, randomly fired across the hangar. Some caught other troopers, pinning them to the walls and floor. Emily zipped aside as a bunch of bullets slammed into the ceiling.

One struck Pete on the side of his leg. Momentum forced the resin-bullet onwards and it ripped a swatch off

Pete's cheap jeans and hit the wall. But the impact was enough to spin him around. He had been busy blasting a group of guards running to the gold-carrier, presumably to use the craft's gun on them - his laser strayed across the floor, ripping through the hose that was refuelling the Hercules. Liquid spurted across the floor in every direction.

Pete slid his glasses back onto his nose and looked at devastation he'd caused. 'Oh no!'

Toby circled again, performing lazy barrel rolls like the fighter aircraft he'd piloted on his computer. The glue-bullets pinged all around him. He saw a handful of goons run towards the rack of glyder-discs.

'No you don't!' he roared and a monstrous fireball shot out across the cavern and hit the glyder rack. The effect was devastating; the remaining glyder-discs were blown to smithereens, the whole rack toppling down on the men who were running towards it. Flames swelled as the structure crashed against the deck, the fire spreading to a number of wooden crates stacked against the wall. Toby cheered triumphantly, then noticed the fuel hose pouring fluid across the floor. Already some soldiers were running away, slipping in the slick avgas that pooled under the Hercules and trickled towards the blazing glyder rack.

'Watch out!' bellowed Toby.

But a deafening siren drowned his warning out. The alarm had finally been raised.

Doc Tempest stood in front of a set of eight giant plasma screens. Each showed the close-up of a world leader, all members of the world's powerful G8, and all of who regarded Tempest with steely defiance. Currently the President of the United States was speaking.

'We know you're bluffin', Bucket-head. So we say no to your demands, and if you don't return our gold reserves then you'll have one big war headin' your way!'

Doc Tempest was apoplectic. He yelled at the screens, spittle flying from his mouth. But his words were lost as a siren filled the command room. He furiously waved at a technician, shouting at her to stop the alarm, but he couldn't be heard. Exasperated, Tempest wheeled around and fired an electrical bolt from his fingers, blasting the alarm-speaker on the ceiling and plunging the command centre into silence. Tempest stabbed a finger at the screens.

'You'll pay for you insolence, Mister President! Say goodbye to Washington D.C.!'

Tempest stabbed a button on his wristband to cut the video transmission. He turned on the cowering technicians.

'What the he—' he stopped, suddenly aware the eight world leaders were still staring at him. Tempest stabbed the button again, several times. This time the screens went blank. He turned again to the technician.

'What is happening?'

'Er... we have intruders in the hangar? And your prisoners have, um, escaped,' squeaked the young technician. He called up a video feed from the security cameras. Doc Tempest gazed venomously at the screen; Toby, Pete and Emily could be seen darting around the hangar, which was already well aflame.

'I'll deal with them! The rest of you, activate the Storm Engine, make the skies boil with fire! Annihilate Washington D.C.!'

With a flourish of his cape, Doc Tempest strode from the

room, though the effect was spoilt when the piecing intruder alarm filled the command centre as the doors slid open.

'And turn that damned alarm off!'

In the space of a few seconds the fuel had already covered half the distance to the blazing fire. Toby swooped down towards Pete, who had discovered that he could fire smaller laser blasts by blinking quickly, but that made him dizzy. Pete dropped onto the mezzanine level, gripping the rail for support. Toby landed next to him.

'Pete! We've got to stop the flames or the aircraft will explode! That's our ticket out with mum!'

'No problem!' said Pete cockily... then he hesitated. 'How?'

'What's your other power? We've got four remember? Forget teleporting and flying, I have fireballs and can grow larger. What can you do?'

Pete set his jaw firmly. It was up to him to save the day. 'You're right! Let's see!'

He slid his glasses back on and extended his hands towards the fuel. The superpower welled up—

And a stream of bubbles issued from his fingers, floating daintily in the air, caught in the thermal updraft of the raging fires below. Toby's mouth opened in shock.

'Bubbles? What kind of stupid superpower is that? Bubbles?

'Well I didn't know!' protested Pete. He thought back to what Chameleon had said about there being no useless powers, and wondered what possible use bubble could provide. Below them, Lorna suddenly became visible again, her hands glowing.

'Will you two stop messing around?' She didn't notice a mercenary was almost upon her, wielding a heavy wrench.

BLAM! The mercenary was suddenly struck sideways and to the floor as a glue-bullet hit him squarely on the side of the head. Lorna looked around to see her mother, wielding the rifle.

'I felt like I wasn't helping out enough,' said Sarah apologetically.

A set of doors at ground level opened and Doc Tempest strode into the hangar. Lightning bolts surged from his fingers in the vain hope he'd accidentally catch one of the young heroes. Instead he did little more than electrocute two of his own men.

'It ends here, kiddies!' bellowed Doc Tempest.

'Watch out!' screamed Toby. He wasn't looking at Tempest but the fuel, which had now reached the burning crates and glyder rack. Blue flames rapidly fanned across the floor in two directions, one towards the split fuel hose that was still attached to the large fuel dump against the wall, and the other towards the Hercules.

The flames reached them both at the same time.

Doc Tempest had barely taken a step before the fuel tank erupted in an orange mushroom cloud that consumed the entire back wall. The blast threw Tempest across the hangar, where a wall of ice collapsed around him.

Emily had been watching everything, and had noticed Lorna and Sarah were too close to the fuel tank. She bolted forward came to an abrupt halt in front of them - using her metal body to protect them from the blast. Their world turned into a torrent of fire, as flames roared all around, but Emily shielded them from getting burnt.

Nobody could stay on their feet as the hangar shook as if

an earthquake had struck. Massive chunks of ice broke from the ceiling, slamming to the ground. Other ice started melting, sending a light rain across the hangar.

Toby and Pete held on tight as the steel platform shuddered from the blast. They watched as the Hercules blew apart. A flaming section of wing spun towards them, forcing them both to duck and run as it embedded into the wall just above their heads.

Another section shot sidelong into the u-shaped mezzanine walkway and exploded again tearing a huge hole in the ice wall, pulling half of the platform down in a crash of steel girders.

The walkway tilted beneath Toby and Pete - and they hung on for life as they rode the structure all the way to the floor. They sprang clear as the walkway folded with a screech of metal.

All around them the hangar burned. The remaining soldiers had already started fleeing into the side corridor.

Toby spotted his mother, Lorna and Emily heaped on the floor and ran across.

'Mum!' he screamed. 'Lorn! Em?'

They stood up with a groan. The silver coating faded from Emily and she picked herself up, wincing as she stretched her back.

'Emie, you okay?' asked Pete with concern.

'That is going to hurt for *months*,' said Emily.

Lorna helped Sarah stand. Toby was expecting to be shouted at, and braced himself for a torrent of unanswerable questions.

Sarah stared at her son, and then threw herself forward, embracing him in a tight hug he couldn't - and didn't want to - escape from.

'Toby... oh, Toby I love you so much!' She began to cry. Toby could feel the tears welling in his own eyes, but once again choked them back. It wasn't seemly for a superhero to cry, especially at his moment of victory.

Lorna grinned, joining in the hug. Pete and Emily glanced at each other and smiled... but no hug was forthcoming there.

'Guess we can go home now,' said Pete looking around the inferno they have created

A clatter of rubble made them turn. A gloved fist had punched through the mound of ice in the corner of the blazing hangar, and then another.

'Ah... guys?' stammered Pete. 'We've got company!'

They all turned to see Doc Tempest rise from the ice like a scruffy and cold phoenix. His normally pale face was red with rage.

'It's not over, lad! Not by a long shot!'

The lights across the hangar flickered. Tempest glanced at them, and then turned back to the group.

'You see, *that* means my Storm Engine is about to power up... and wipe the Capital of the United States clean off the map!'

The four heroes strode forward ready to continue the fight. Doc Tempest's head snapped back as he roared with amusement.

'That's right. You fight me... or you deactivate the weapon and save *millions* of innocent lives. Oooh... the dilemma! What would *real* heroes choose to do?' His sniggering echoed from the destruction around them. Then he started making tick-tock noises.

The heroes exchanged nervous glances, all except Toby. Determination was etched on his face.

'Real heroes would do *both*.' He stepped forward, fists clenched. Without taking his eyes off Tempest he spoke to the others. 'Lorna, you know where the Storm Engine is?'

'Yeah, we can stop it.'

'Good, take mum with you. Pete, go with them!'

Pete began to protest. 'But—'

'Trust me. I have a really *big* idea.'

Pete instantly understood. 'Come on, guys. Toby's got this covered. Lorna, lead the way!'

They hesitated, but Pete urged them across the hangar towards the door Lorna had pointed to. Sarah cast one last look at her son, squaring up to the Supervillain.

'Toby! Be careful!' she screamed.

Pete gently pushed her forward. 'Don't worry, Mrs Wilkinson. He's got things in hand.'

Doc Tempest watched the others disappear from the hangar then turned his puzzled glance to Toby.

'Is this some kind of joke?' he rumbled. 'You dare to try and ruin my entire scheme and then think I would have issues with crushing a *boy*?'

'No joke. Just you and me! But before I humiliate you... just one thing. What *did* happen to your head?'

The condescending look on Doc Tempest's face faded. 'I will make you wish you'd never been born when you feel my wrath!'

What he wasn't prepared for was to see Toby suddenly *grow*. It all happened very quickly. First his hands swelled to three times their normal size; then the effect spread along his arms. His body, head and legs swiftly followed to a chorus of ripping clothes.

Doc Tempest raised his hands to fire a lightning bolt, but he hesitated in alarm when he saw that the boy was twice as

large as the supervillain, with muscles popping under the
ribbons of clothing that still clung to his skin and hid his
modesty.

Lorna and Emily were running ahead of Pete and Sarah.
Lorna spoke low to her friend.

'I had a thought. Maybe my mother should, you know…
forget about all of this once we get home?'

Emily gave her a meaningful glance and nodded.

'Hey guys,' shouted Pete, already out of breath.
'Wouldn't this be quicker flying?'

'Er… I can't fly,' said Sarah.

Pete and Emily hooked an arm each under Sarah's
armpits and took her weight.

'I don't know how to do this!' complained Sarah.

'It's easy,' said Pete. 'All you have to do is miss the
ground!'

Bam! It was like running into a mountain. Doc Tempest staggered back from Toby, slightly dazed. Toby tried to rush him
again, but this time Tempest dropped down and away. Toby
swung a huge fist, but it was too slow, allowing Tempest just
enough time to roll aside.

Doc Tempest jumped to his feet, arms extended; lightning bolts gushed from his fingers and struck Giant Toby.
Toby reeled back - it hurt, like being stuck by pins. But in his
giant form, it didn't hurt anywhere near as much as it should.

Tempest stopped in surprise, and Toby took a thun-
derous step forward, suddenly aware he was wading through
water. The fires were melting the ice on the walls and ceiling.

Cracks began to spread across the walls and roof with alarming speed. Small pieces of ice were raining down.

Doc Tempest looked up to watch his precious Antarctic base crumble around him - and didn't see Toby's backhand that connected with him. Tempest reeled backwards, rubbing the side of his head.

Toby bore down on Tempest in a fury of punches. 'That's for my mother! And that one's for demolishing my house!'

The final punch walloped Tempest's jaw, and the villain skidded along the hangar floor in a spray of icy water.

Spittle flew from Toby's mouth as he lost his temper. 'And that's for making my life hell!'

Doc Tempest rubbed his jaw, and then raised his hand as Toby lumbered towards him. His anger had made Toby drop his guard - it was just the opportunity that Tempest was waiting for.

A stream of ice leapt from Tempest's fingers and smothered Toby, freezing him to the spot like an ice sculpture.

They flew down the corridors, occasionally bouncing from the walls as they took a corner wide. There was no sign of guards in the corridor, which gently spiralled up the cone of the mountain. A familiar double sliding door appeared ahead.

'This is it!' said Lorna.

'I'll go first!' shouted Pete, pushing his glasses back on his head and leaping into the room.

The Storm Engine was glowing with a radiant energy, and the humming from it was steadily rising in pitch. The glass canopy of the mountain peak had opened on hydraulic arms, and a bitterly cold wind was blowing inside, with it flurries of snow.

The technicians were still here, and hadn't heard the new arrivals as they all wore ear-protectors and were staring fixedly at the Weapon of Mass Destruction.

'Nobody move!' bellowed Pete.

Nobody could hear him. Pete aimed his laser vision with a series of short pulses that blew up several of the control consoles. The technicians spun around, pulling their ear-protectors away.

'Nobody move,' repeated Pete who was disappointed his initial dramatic entrance had passed unheard. To emphasise his point, he shot a bundle of cables with his laser vision. But that seemed to increase the tempo of the machine. The technicians raised their hands in surrender, quickly shuffling to the far corner of the room, away from the machine.

'Er... how do we stop it?'

'Let me try!' shouted Emily.

She took to the air and allowed her skin to flow into liquid metal once again. Then she flew for the heart of the Storm Engine—

The central column detonated in a huge white flash as she passed through - the tip of the dish blew apart in a more traditionally satisfying explosion.

The technicians charged from the room in panic.

Lorna landed back with her friends as further eruptions rocked the Storm Engine. The pitch of the machine was now building to ear-screeching proportions.

'It's going to blow!' shouted Emily. 'We better get out of here!'

'How?' shouted Pete as the floor began to buck. 'I... er... somebody blew up the plane, and that was our ticket out!'

'We'll have to try to teleport!' screamed Lorna as the noise grew in intensity.

'Can we teleport your mum,' yelled Emily. 'She's got no superpowers!'

'We have to try!'

'Not without Toby!' Pete screamed back. A wide crack shot along the ice floor between Pete's legs, forcing him to hop aside.

'We know where he is - we're not leaving him behind!' replied Lorna, throwing her arms around her mother, who momentarily mistook it as a sign of affection.

'It's okay...' Sarah began soothingly.

'Grab my mum! We're leaving!'

Pete and Emily threw their arms around Sarah, and concentrated *hard*...

Doc Tempest was on his feet, and wobbling precariously as the ground shook beneath him and ice rained down with increasing frequency. He stared at frozen Toby with malice.

'You can't defeat me, boy! I've been in this game too long. I know all your tricks!'

Tempest began advancing, sploshing through the ankle-deep water. Toby felt the stabbing chill of his ice prison. It was made worse because he was half naked, wearing shredded clothing. He only had one choice. He began to tense every muscle in his over-grown body. Massive tendons pushed against the ice—

CRUNCH! The ice cast around Toby shattered pelting wedges at Doc Tempest. Toby stepped from the ice prison.

'I've already beaten you, Tempest!' Toby allowed himself to shrink back to normal size; using one hand to make sure his tattered clothing didn't *all* fall off. 'It's time you surrendered.'

'Your mistake is letting me live!'

With a pop of displaced air, Lorna, Pete, Emily and Sarah suddenly appeared in the hangar.

'It works!' shouted Pete excitedly. 'We can teleport your mum! But we have to leave *now*! This whole place is about to explode!'

A house-sized slab of the roof dislodged *directly* above Tempest and Toby. Toby sprung away as hard as he could. He heard Tempest bellow his name—

The fiend raised his arms in a pathetic attempt to stop the block as it struck the floor in a colossal splash of water. Tempest was pinned underneath, legs crushed. He reached pathetically out.

'Help me... please,' he said in a hoarse voice.

Toby felt oddly numb. He had no desire to save the fiend, but knew it was the right thing to do.

'Like I said: I've already beaten you.'

Toby took a step forward to help Tempest, but noticed that the villain had extended his arms for a last lightning strike. Toby saw the electrical charge manifest in Tempest's hand - at the exact moment he felt an arm move around his waist—

The lightning bolt fizzled the air where Toby *had* been standing. The heroes had all teleported away.

Amid the fire and falling ice, Tempest was too weak to even curse.

From the vast, barren planes of the Antarctic it seemed as if an entire peak of one of the mountains exploded in a miniature mushroom cloud. But the flames soon faded as freezing winds smothered the mountains with more snow.

They had been home for a day, falling instantly asleep as their heads touched their beds, and just in time too, as their superpowers had run out almost within minutes of returning. Emily's parents had insisted Sarah could stay until she could sort things out with her own home.

Sarah had fully recovered from her diabetic attack and had no recollection of what had happened after the twister struck her home. Her best guess was that she must have been carried away by the freak tornado and dropped unconscious some distance away. She had no memory of *anything* other than waking on the sofa in Emily's house.

Toby and Pete were a little puzzled by this, until Lorna took them aside and explained that Emily's mind-control power had blanked the events from her mind.

The secret of the Hero community was safe.

Toby recalled Chameleon's words about the path of a hero. They had overcome danger, and had learnt to work together as a team. The danger and risks had been worth it.

Lorna once more voiced her idea that they should use their powers to do some high profile heroic work that would get them on a TV chat show. Emily was more cautious; she preferred keeping a lid on things. At least until they had a little more experience. This caused a heated discussion between the three friends.

Only Pete kept quiet. He was wrestling with his own thoughts. On the one hand he was revelling that he had superpowers, but returning home to his parents ongoing and increasingly bitter arguments shadowed that thrill, as did the knowledge that he would be bullied again at school. It was a real downer for a hero to face. If only he could think of a way to change things.

On the TV they watched as news reports came in that the stolen U.S. Government gold had been found in Antarctica, and was currently being retrieved. Although, apparently, there was no sign of the thieves.

All four of the heroes sat in Emily's kitchen, nursing their bruises and feeling immense pride over their achievements. Then Sarah came rushing into the room, sobbing.

'Mum... what's the matter?' asked Toby anxiously. He prayed she had not suddenly remembered her children flying around, shooting fireballs and turning invisible.

'It's your father,' she said, between sobs. 'He was returning from his dig. We've just heard reports about his plane... it has developed mechanical trouble... and they don't think it can land! He's going to crash!'

Pete mumbled under his breath. 'Why is your family *always* in danger?'

As Emily's parents consoled Sarah, Pete and Toby exchanged glances and they all rose from their chairs.

'We just need to use the computer... for homework,' said Pete.

The adults ignored the children as they left the room. After all, this was a *real* problem, what could the children possibly hope to achieve on the *Internet*?

END NOTES_

info@andybriggsbooks.com

or say hello on Twitter:

@abriggswriter

NEXT IN THE SERIES:

.

.

.

Or the parallel series:

Parallel series? What is that?

Watch as characters make **CAMEOS** and **AFFECT THE PLOT** of the book you've just read! The stories are interlinked and happen roughly at the same time - you will even see some surprising character arcs that only come to life between the separate series. You may even see scenes that happen **OFF THE PAGE** of the other book.

Of course, the series can be enjoyed separately too!

YOUNG ADULT

MARLOW

HERO 1: RISE OF THE HEROES
HERO 2: VIRUS ATTACK
HERO 3: CRISIS POINT
HERO 4: CHAOS EFFECT

VILLAIN 1: COUNCIL OF EVIL
VILLAIN 2: DARK HUNTER
VILLAIN 3: POWER SURGE
VILLAIN 4: COLLISION COURSE

ADULT THRILLERS

EPICENTER
CHEM (February 2021)
PHANTOM LAND (April 2021)

By Orion

CTRL+S

Young Adult Books: By Scholastic

DRONE RACER

THE INVENTORY: IRON FIST

THE INVENTORY: GRAVITY

THE INVENTORY: BLACK KNIGHT

THE INVENTORY: WINTER STORM

By Faber

TARZAN: THE GREYSTOKE LEGACY

TARZAN: THE JUNGLE WARRIOR

TARZAN: THE SAVAGE LANDS

By Hachette

WARRIOR NUMBER ONE

By Lonely Planet (non-fiction)

HOW TO BE AN INTERNATIONAL SPY

Graphic Novels by Markosia

DINOCORPS

RITUAL

RITUAL: RESURRECTION

MEAT

Printed in Great Britain
by Amazon

19248552R00130